Chasing Ghosts

Book Two in the Always Forward Series

Cecilia A. Garcia

Cecilia A. Garcia

Content Warning

Chasing Ghosts is a fictional novella with graphic content that depicts combat scenes, post-traumatic stress flashbacks, and sexual trauma. There are also vivid descriptions of injuries that may be difficult for some readers. If you or someone you know is dealing with a type of trauma or this book uncovers the trauma you, the reader, need to deal with, know that you are not alone. Please reach out to the Mental Health America crisis line at 1-800-273-TALK (8255) or text MHA to 741741 at the Crisis Text Line.

Chasing Ghosts is dedicated to all service members
that have made the ultimate sacrifice.
~Until Valhalla.

Table of Contents

Chapter One

EMILY

———◇———

My eyes feel heavy, and my body feels like what skin I have left on my bones is being shredded with every move it makes. I can still hear those voices, speaking in Arabic, yelling, gunshots, more screaming. I try to lift my arms, but I can't lift them from my sides. I try again, and it occurs to me that someone has tied my arms to my sides. My eyes are so heavy; I try to focus, but they can't seem to see anything. But the voices, they are all around me, as if they are surrounding me as if I could get away. I try to open my mouth but realize it's taped shut. I'm now in complete panic, and I begin to try and twist and turn. When my eyes start to focus, I see a hand coming down towards my face to hit me.

I hear explosions going off around me, and I begin to roll back and forth from my stomach to my back. No, no, no, stop! I grab my head; the explosions will not stop. I feel the ground shake around me, and I don't know if I was in the hole back when I was first captured or the present. I go back to when they were dragging me through the street. I couldn't see in focus, but I knew what was happening to me. I could feel the rough patches of the dirt road as somebody dragged me through the streets. A few times when my eyes did focus between blows, I think I saw Grant. Oh, Grant! His body was mangled and bloodied. I hoped he was dead for his own sake because there would be no way that anyone could survive the way his body looked. Then again, how many times had I wished I would die.

More explosions and yelling. I can't decipher if the yelling is in Arabic or not, but I crawl to the far corner of my hole and put myself into the tightest ball I can. I tuck my head into my knees and pray that this is the end. Please, Lord, I have been through so much; just let this be the end. The explosions stop, but a firefight then begins. I continue to keep my head tucked into my knees, rocking back and forth, waiting for the monster to open the hatch and kill me.

Sometime later, the gunfire slows down, and then it stops altogether. I feel a draft and then see a sliver of daylight coming down into the hole as someone opens the hatch. I try to fade into the rear wall of the cavity, but there is nowhere else for me to go. I remember the first time I woke up here and how I did the same movement back then. I see a pair of combat boots land in the hole, and it does not look like the monster, Mahir, or any of the other soldiers that work for him. The combat boots land, and I look up into the face of an American soldier. Tears well up in my eyes, and I wipe them away with the back of my hand.

"Are you Sgt. Emily Sanders?" He doesn't move from where he landed in the hole, and I can tell he is trying to be cautious with his movements. I stare at him because I genuinely do not know if this is real or one of my dreams slash nightmares.

"Are you Sgt. Emily Sanders? I need you to answer me. Nod your head yes if you are Sgt. Sanders." I slowly nod my head as I stare into this soldier's dark brown eyes. He begins to move slowly, removing his right arm from the sling of his weapon attached to the front of his chest. I can't stop staring at his weapon. He slowly begins to walk towards me, and he has to bend over to walk in the hole. "I'm going to reach forward and help you out of here. My name is SFC Montoya, and I have a team of guys just outside of here waiting to help you. Do I have your permission to touch you?"

I nod my head yes again, and he begins to walk towards me slowly. I scan his uniform, and I know he is an American soldier by the flag on his arm, but I don't recognize the uniform. He makes his way over to me and stops right in front of me, and kneels. SFC Montoya moves forward slowly and begins to put his arms around me. I open my arms up to embrace him. I don't mean to hug him, but I do. SFC Montoya is the first human contact I have had in who knows how long. I still can't believe this is happening, and, in some ways, I wonder if this is a dream. But I can feel his body and his arms around me. I can smell the soap he used probably before leaving on this mission on his skin. He is real, and he is getting me out of here.

He picks me up in his arms as though I weigh nothing at all. "Okay, Sgt. Sanders, I am going to have to lift you now. There will be another soldier at the top of the opening that will pull you out of here. We are getting you out of here, I promise." Montoya gives me a solemn nod, and I know I can trust him. I finally find my voice, "Okay, I am ready." I say weakly. He lifts me, and I use my arms to reach up out of the hole. There is another soldier lowered on their stomach, ready to pull me out. It registers that this soldier is a female, which surprises me, but I don't have time to dwell on it. She drags me out of the hole, and I feel the dirt rub against my skin, and I don't care about the pain. My rescue is happening. It's not a dream.

As this new soldier pulls me out, there is another explosion nearby. I can't make out if they are RPGs or not. But they are loud, and they are close. The soldier scoops me up, and I wrap my arms around her neck. There is so much smoke and debris in the air that I bury my face into her Kevlar vest. I can hear her talking through the vest. She is radioing into the rest of the group that she has Sgt. Sanders.

She has me. I hold on even tighter, not wanting to let go of her.

I was ready to fight my way out, but after Mahir brought water that first time, no one had come back for me. It's almost as though they planned to let me rot to death in that hole. I had tried to claw my way out like I had all those years before, but it had been no use. With no food and very little water left, I had no energy to try to scale the mud-caked walls of the hole. I'm not even sure how long I had been asleep before I heard the explosions begin. I squeeze my savior even more as we start to move.

"Don't worry, Sarge," the soldier says, "We are going to get you out of here." I begin to weep quietly into her vest. I do not want her to see my tears of gratitude.

This new soldier begins to jog while cradling me in her arms. I keep my face tucked into her vest not only because of the smoke and dirt flying around in the air but because I do not want to see the monster. I genuinely hope he is dead. But then a new round of panic hits my chest. I don't want Mahir dead. I know that he is a good human; it's not his fault he was born to a monster and forced to believe whatever thoughts the monster put in his head. God, I hope he is safe with the other children. I hold on a little tighter to the soldier as she picks up her pace. She acts as though I weigh nothing at all, and maybe that's true. When she begins to slow down, I lift my head a little bit to see. The smoke begins to thin out, and there have not been any explosions or gunfire for some time now. I look around and see the village in front of us. It is a complete ghost town even though it seems to be the middle of the day. I remember from my early deployment days that this was standard protocol for the locals. Whenever they knew danger was coming, they ran to their safe havens and hid until there was an all-clear sign. I hoped no innocent villagers were injured or killed. But who was innocent? The village knew who I was and what the monster had been doing to me for all these years. Why did I want them safe if they could have helped me?

The soldier begins to slow down to a jog and then starts walking. I see past the huts, and there is a helicopter waiting for us. The soldier leans her head down to mine so I can hear her, "Sarge, we are going to put you on this chopper with another crew. There is a female medic on board who is going to take care of you. I am going to have to lay you down on a stretcher when we get closer, and they will be strapping you down for safety. Do you understand?" I nod my head and look up at her. This strong soldier doesn't look much older than Malika. "Yes, I understand. But I have children here. What will happen to them?" The soldier has an exceptional poker face, considering how young she is. "That is why we are staying back. We need to ensure the village is safe and gather your children. I promise you they will be safe."

"Thank you," I say to the soldier. I realize she never told me her name, and with all her gear on, I can't see the name tape. We approached the helicopter, and she was correct. There is a team of soldiers waiting, one of which is a female. She lays me down on the stretcher, and I lift my right hand to her and grab on to her sleeve. "Wait!" I yell at her over the blades of the helicopter. "I didn't get your name, soldier." She grabs onto my hand and squeezes it tight, "I am Specialist Belka, Sarge. And it was an honor to help you today." With that, she drops my hand and takes off before I can muster out a thank you. Specialist Belka. I will never forget her, and if I truly get out of this country, I make a vow to myself to find her again.

Chapter Two

TARA

Tara was sleeping when Doc's wife woke her up. She tells Tara to get dressed and come to Doc's office. Tara scrambles to get up and gets dressed quickly in the dark. Her heart was pounding in her chest; even though she wasn't sure what was going on, she knew it had to be about her mom. Tara jogs across the medical village to Doc's office. She notices right away several military Humvees parked by the entrance gate. Tara's heart begins to pound harder in her chest, and she tries to take a
deep breath as she walks into Doc's tent.

The two men she had met last time were in the tent, along with several other soldiers. This time the Lieutenant and Sergeant were in uniform, and all five of them had on their tactical gear as if they were ready for combat. Doc stood up from his desk where he had been looking over a map with 1LT Gomez. Doc takes a deep breath and places his hands on his hips. "Well, Tara, there is no easy way to say this but, the government has given the Army the all-clear to move forward with evacuating your mother."

Tara stares at Doc, not understanding why he looks so grave when he just delivered the best news to her ever. "Okay, this is great news! When do we leave to get her?" Tara widens her stance as if she will have to face off in a fistfight.

1LT Gomez takes a step forward and stares straight into Tara's eyes. "Look, Tara, we know that you want to help and that you want to be there when we rescue your mother. But the situation has escalated to a potential combative threat." he pauses as if he knows Tara will have questions about that last part. "Escalated to a potential combative threat?" Tara repeats, trying not to let the octave in her voice raise any higher. "So, what you're saying is that your suspicions were correct about the insurgents? Does that mean my mom's life is in critical danger? Is there a chance the insurgents might kill my mom before I even have a chance to see her again?" As Tara asked the last question, she couldn't hold back the tears. They fell freely down her cheeks.

Doc came over to stand next to Tara and began to rub her back. "Tara," Doc says as he draws circles on her back. "You know the answer to that. We are always in danger over here. But yes, depending on how the operation goes for these men depends on if we can evacuate your mom safely."

Tara swallowed hard, even though her throat was dry. She nodded her head to show that she understood. Even though her dad had talked in-depth about the dangers of Iraq even during peacetime, hearing Doc and the Special Forces team discuss it made it feel so real. There was a chance the insurgents could kill the team and her mom during the rescue. She closed her eyes and then reopened them and looked 1LT Gomez directly in the eyes. "Okay, sir. What do you need me to do?"

The men explained to Tara that she would be evacuated from the medical village, flown to Baghdad by helicopter, and then flown to Kuwait. They could not risk having her nearby in case the insurgents discovered that she was Emily's daughter. Tara went through the motions of agreeing when she had to and asking questions when she felt they were waiting for her to inquire about something. But all she could think about was her mom. She silently prayed that these men who trained for these missions would safely get her out of here.

Tara left the tent with clear instructions. She had an hour to pack her bags and say a quick goodbye to Nick and Rosie. Tara's instructions were to not share any details with them, except that she was flying out of the village for personal reasons. Lucky for her, both Nick and Rosie were clever enough to read between the lines when she explained this to them both. Nick brought her in for a tight embrace and kissed her deeply. "I love you, Tara, with my entire heart and soul."

Tara squeezed Nick even harder, worried that he and everyone left at the village may be in danger. The Special Forces team had assured her that there would be security at the medical village. But she was still worried, not just for Nick and Rosie but the entire medical team. After all, they were a family, and if the insurgents would harm anyone because of her initiative to find her mom, Tara wasn't sure if she could ever live with herself. "I love you too, Nick." They kissed one more time, and then Tara pulled apart from their embrace.

Tara then shared with Rosie that she was leaving and whispered to her how grateful she had opened up to Rosie about her mom. Even though she couldn't share any details, Rosita understood and squeezed Tara tightly as they said their goodbyes. Her hour was up, and it was time to go. All she could do now was wait patiently for the call that the Special Forces had her mom safe and sound.

Tara walked back to Doc's tent with her two bags slung over her shoulder. SFC Matthews was waiting by one of the Humvees for her. When he saw her approach, he quickly put out the cigarette he had been smoking. "You know, Sergeant, those things will kill you." Tara smiled at him as she threw her bags into the back of the Humvee. SFC Matthews gave her a small smile and nodded his head as he fields stripped the cigarette butt and slid it into his pocket.

"I quit about five years ago if you ask my wife. But I still smoke every time we are getting ready to take care of business." With that, the smile he had flashed her was gone, and a serious look reappeared on his face. "Tara, I don't know your mom personally, but I know your dad. I was a young infantryman when he was working through the details of planning your mom's funeral. I looked up to your dad, shit I still do. He was and is still a fine leader. A lot of us remember him and everything he has been through over the last decade. I'm not going to let anything happen to your mom. You have my word that I will bring your mom home to you and your dad." SFC Matthews placed his hand out palm facing up. Tara took his hand, and they stood there in silence.

Tara cleared her throat because she felt the tears getting ready to fall any second now. "In the words of my mother, always forward Sergeant First Class Matthews. The only way to go from here is always forward." Tara knew she might never see SFC Matthews or 1LT Gomez again, but she would never forget them for not only believing in her but following through with the rescue operation. She knew that if SFC Matthews were giving her his solemn vow to get her mom out of here, then he would do whatever it took to stay true to his vow.

Chapter Three

JOSH

◆─◇─◆

As Josh finished up yet another early morning run, he walked up to his driveaway, arms on top of his head to help cool him off quicker. He was still waking up around 0300 every morning after having the same replay dream over and over again. Josh still couldn't shake that nothing was wrong, but when he had reached out to his contacts in Iraq, they confirmed that everyone at the medical village was safe and nothing unusual had been going on. When he asked if they could get a message to Tara, they said they would try, but she was going to Kuwait on a supply run. Even with this reassurance that everything was okay, he still had felt a continued uneasiness. It made no sense, especially since Alicia had just gotten back from her missionary trip in the Caribbean. She was safe at home; Tara was safe in Kuwait. So, where were all these feelings of impending doom coming from for him?

Josh sat on the steps of his front porch as he did after every run. He unlaced his shoes and placed them off to the side. Josh took his phone out of his armband, turning it on after finishing his run. He never ran with music on and began turning it off to be distracted by calls and texts. He only carried it to keep Dina and the girls from worrying about him since he loved to run so early in the morning. Once his phone turned on, the notifications began flooding in. Missed call after missed call. They just kept populating on his screen. All numbers he didn't recognize, more than likely government numbers. His heart began to pound, thinking that something terrible may have happened to Tara. Once the missed calls stopped, the voicemails were the next slew of notifications to fill the screen. Now he knew something was wrong. He clicked on the most recent voicemail. It is a First Lieutenant from a Special Forces unit. He is not familiar with the name, but then again, he has been out for a few years, and this officer sounds young.

Josh almost drops the phone as the officer recites the words he believed he would never hear. "MSG Sanders, we have confirmed that SGT Emily Sanders is alive. Your daughter Tara aided in identifying your wife. They are both safe and are on their way to Landstuhl, Germany. You will not be able to reach us, as these satellite phones will not receive incoming calls. We will contact you as soon as we land and can provide additional details."

Emily is alive. Josh stared at his phone as the voicemail ended. His vision became blurry, and a buzzing sound had begun around him. Emily is alive. How? Where? What had happened to even get to this point? Tara. He hadn't believed Tara and her gut instincts all these years. He hadn't wanted her to go to Iraq because he genuinely thought she would come home with a broken heart for trying to find a ghost. But she had been right. Emily is alive.

Josh listens to several of the older voicemails, but they all had been the same 1LT Gomez, but with fewer details. The Lieutenant must have had to go and had made the judgment call to release classified information on a voicemail. Not precisely standard operating procedures, but Josh would let it slide. His Emily was alive. He sat there staring off into the distance, not sure what to do next. The Lieutenant had stated they would contact him as soon as they were able to. Until then, he had no additional details to share with anyone. This news was like the reverse of finding out when Emily had gone missing. Instead of calling her parents to tell them she was gone, he had to tell Emily's mom now she was alive. God, they had buried an empty casket. She had a headstone, for Christ's sake. What the hell? How would he explain to her that he had given up on her? That he had buried her and the life they had six feet below the ground. And Dina. What does he tell Dina? How would she react to the news?

Not able to handle all the thoughts in his head, he stood up and began pacing on the porch. He determined he couldn't call Emily's mom until he had more information. He knew her mom would have tons of questions, just like he did. No, he would wait and call her once he heard from 1LT Gomez. He also determined he didn't want to tell Dina yet. Same with her, she would have more questions than Josh would have answers. Plus, he was still wrapping his head around what this meant for their marriage. Josh loved Dina, she was an amazing woman, but Emily had been his soulmate. He would never have left Emily for another woman in a million years if Emily had never gone missing. He couldn't wrap his head around if this meant he was legally married to two women at once?

He stopped pacing, staring at his phone still in his hand. "Dammit, all to hell," Josh said as he looked up to the roof of the porch. He went into his contacts and called the only person he knew that not only would understand him not having any answers but also deserved to know before anyone else. The last person who saw Emily alive was Rodriguez. He hit call and brought the phone up to his ear. After several rings, a raspy male voice comes through the other end. "This better be my wake-up call that you have breakfast cooking, and I should head on over for a plate full of your steaming biscuits and gravy." Rodriguez loves Josh's breakfast cooking and typically invites himself over for Josh to cook for him. When Josh doesn't say anything right away, Josh can hear Rodriguez sitting up in bed. "Sanders, what's up, man? Is everything okay? Are you there?" Now Rodriguez has panic in his voice, and Josh knows he has to find the words to say. But he hasn't said them out loud yet, and he's afraid he's going to break down crying to one of his closest friends over the phone.

"EMILY IS ALIVE!" Josh blurts the words out, and they come out more in a shout than a normal tone. "WHAT?" Rodriguez asks Josh in disbelief. "Are you fucking serious right now?" He asks, now going to a more hushed tone, probably so he doesn't disturb his wife. "Yes, I am 100% serious right now. I just got back from my run and had a million missed calls and voicemails. They found Emily alive, and she and Tara are on their way to Germany." Josh takes a deep breath, finds one of the chairs on the porch, and takes a seat. All of a sudden, his legs felt like Jell-O, and everything began to be blurry again.

"Okay, dude, I am headed over. I want you to go inside and start making breakfast. We need to eat and talk this out." Rodriguez dished out the commands over the phone, and Josh gladly took them. He was in no place to make any other decisions or talk to anyone else at the moment. "Roger that Rodriguez." And with that, Josh ended the call. He knew Dina was inside, probably finishing up her workout and getting ready for work. Josh felt like a total jerk, but he would have to keep this news from her until he learned more. Plus, he needed to process this more and talk it out with Rodriguez. And he knew Rodriguez was right; eating and talking always worked best for the two of them.

Josh headed into the house, and sure enough, he could hear the shower going. He went to the kitchen and began gathering everything he needed for his famous biscuits and gravy. Josh felt terrible making Dina her standard shake, but she wouldn't have time to stick around for the bigger meal to be done. He made a mental note to make sure he saved her some for leftovers. Dina came out a little while later, and Josh could sense that Dina knew something wasn't quite right. But luckily for him, she didn't press him to share. She simply grabbed her coffee and protein shake, gave him a quick peck on the cheek, and headed to the garage to leave for work. He kept working on the gravy, but it sounded as though Dina had paused before going through the door to the garage. He looked over his shoulder and gave her a big smile, "Love you, sweetie!" He said with more of a forced cheer than was needed. "Love you too, Josh." She smiled, not quite so big, and headed out.

A few minutes after Dina pulled out of the driveway, Josh heard Rodriguez pull in. No need to let him in; Rodriguez would take care of that on his own. Rodriguez walked in slowly, leaning on his cane more than he usually did. Josh tried not to stare as he walked over to the kitchen island and took a seat.

Josh continued plating their breakfast, two biscuits, a shit ton of gravy, and a spoonful of scrambled eggs. They sat there in silence for a few minutes while Josh finished up. Finally, Rodriguez broke the silence.

"Alright, Sanders, let's hear it. How the hell is this even possible?" Rodriguez grabbed the plate offered him and waited for Josh to respond. Josh shook his head as he sat down across from Rodriguez. "I have no idea, man. All I know is that I got back from my run this morning and had a ton of missed calls and voicemails. It was a ıLT Gomez from Special Forces, and he said that Sgt. Emily Sanders was alive, and she and Tara were on their way to Germany." God, repeating it seemed so crazy. Emily is alive, and Josh still couldn't wrap his head around it.

Rodriguez stopped eating and let his fork hit the plate. "Bro, you know that is not what I mean. I meant, how the hell could she have been alive for over a fucking decade and the Army never found her?" Josh could hear the anger rising in his voice. Since Rodriguez had been an 88M, a transportation specialist, he wasn't involved in the search and rescue missions. Shit, even though Josh had been in Special Forces, he had not even been involved since his wife was missing. His chain of command felt he was too close to the MIA soldier to be involved in the operations. He remembered how helpless he felt every time he would receive another call to let him know the guys leading another search and rescue had come up empty-handed.

Josh sighed and chose his words carefully, not wanting to start an argument with one of his closest friends. "I don't know, Cam." Rodriguez looked up; Josh never called him by his shortened first name. They always went by their last names, but it came out because Josh felt a lot of emotions coming on, and last names weren't cutting it at the moment. "I have no idea how she could have been out there all these years, and we had no fucking clue. I mean, I buried an empty casket for Christ's sake. How the fuck could I do that to her?" Josh's voice had begun to crack, and he felt a wave of guilt flooding over him. He cleared his throat and kept going, the floodgates now open; there was no stopping it now.

"Not only did I bury her and walk away, but I also got fucking married again. I fell in love with another fucking woman. How did I let this happen?" Josh looked across at Rodriguez; his buddy stared back at him.

"You weren't alone in burying her, Josh. Don't ever forget that. We all walked away from her because the fucking Army told us we had to. Our fucking Army told us to give up on her, and we did. Don't you dare carry this burden alone? Do you hear me? Simmons did that and look where he's at now." Josh closed his eyes and thought about Simmons. He had been the other survivor in the Humvee and had been the one that told Rodriguez that Emily was dead. After several attempts to get Emily out of the burning vehicle, Rodriguez had listened to Simmons only to have a small arms fire begin again. Simmons and Rodriguez had taken a shot, Simmons in the right knee cap, Rodriguez in his calf. Simmons couldn't walk at all, so Rodriguez had dragged him to safety. Simmons had survived, but a few years later, he took his own life. He carried the guilt that had he not convinced Rodriguez to stop working on getting Emily out, that maybe she would be alive and safe at home. Simmons' suicide had been another profound loss for Josh and Rodriguez. A few years after that, the Army would call off the search and rescue operations for Emily and Grant. They were both pronounced killed in action, and the date of death was the day of the ambush eight years earlier.

They both silently nodded at each other and finished their meals. The only sounds coming from the kitchen are their forks scraping against the plates. After breakfast, Rodriguez helped Josh clean up, and they both went out to the backyard to sit.

Rodriguez sat down and placed his cane against his leg, rubbing his calf. Josh nodded to Rodriguez's leg. "Still bothering you, huh?"

Rodriguez shrugged and said, "Yeah, it just started to flare up again. Not much I can do for it, you know? I just got to deal with the aches. I'm not complaining, though. I mean, I'm never going to run a marathon, but then again, I'm no Josh Superhero Fucking Sanders, am I?" And this was how their friendship worked. They could go from sharing deep soulful shit to talking shit in the next second. Josh smiled and barked out a laugh. "I guess not everyone can be so lucky to be Josh Sanders, huh?" They fist-bumped and sat there on the back patio, staring out into the woods behind Josh's house.

After quite some time of sitting there in silence, Rodriguez finally began to stand up slowly. "Well, Bro, I'm not sure what else to say or do for the moment. But I do know that if I don't get home soon, my wife is going to straight kick my ass." Josh laughed and got up from his seat too. "I will keep you posted. As soon as I hear something, you will know. And hey, please don't share this news with anyone yet. I haven't told Dina, Alicia, or Emily's mom. Until I have a better understanding and more details, let's plan on keeping this between us." Rodriguez nodded and walked over to Josh. They clasped hands first, but then Rodriguez brought Josh in for a hug. Beating Josh's back, Rodriguez said, "You know I always got your back, Bro. One way or another, we will get through this and figure out what is going on."

Josh closed his eyes, not wanting Rodriguez to know precisely how much he meant to Josh. They let go of each other, and Josh walked Rodriguez out to his car. Josh went back into the house and stood in the living room staring out the floor-length windows into the back yard. Emily is alive and on her way to Germany. Emily. Is. Alive.

Chapter Four

TARA

Tara was back in the same hotel she had begun her Middle Eastern mission on over six months ago. She hadn't stopped pacing for hours, more than likely wearing down the paisley printed carpet beneath her feet. When Tara had first arrived in the country, she had been full of excitement, optimism and was nervous about what was to come. As confident as she had been to her dad and Nick about finding her mom, deep down, she had worried that she was chasing ghosts. She knew that, but she had persisted. Pushing forward like her mom would have done. Now here she was, pacing back and forth in a hotel in Kuwait. SFC Matthews and 1LT Gomez promised her they would contact her as soon as they had information to share with her. It was killing her not to be able to talk to anyone, not even her dad. They had instructed her not to have contact with anyone under any circumstances. They could not take any chances that the insurgents keeping her mom prisoner did not have moles nestled everywhere- from the clinic to the villagers and even here in Kuwait. So, she paced. Making a track from one side of the bed to the other and then back again. Every once in a while, she would stop near her floor-to-ceiling windows and pull back the shades. Life in Kuwait was business as usual. People were going about their day as if everything was just fine. She wanted to scream out from the window, 'DON'T YOU KNOW?? MY MOTHER IS MISSING! MY MOTHER HAS BEEN MISSING FOR OVER 15 YEARS!' But she put the shades back in place and took up her pacing again.

Eventually, Tara laid down on the bed. One wouldn't think pacing in a small hotel room could tire you out, but she was exhausted. Not just physically, but emotionally and mentally too. She drifted off to sleep, dreams fading into memories of growing up with her mom and then without her mom. She dreamt of the day her mom left for Iraq. Tara was little, and the memories were choppy, but they came in and out in her dreams as if she was tuning an old AM radio. In her dreams, she doesn't want to let go of her mom. As much as her mom promised her, Emily would be back soon; in her dream, Tara could feel the impending doom. She squeezes her mom's neck and cries into her shoulder. "Tara Bug, it's going to be okay. I'm just going to go take care of the monsters so they don't make their way under your bed." And then her mom would have to pry Tara's little arms from around her neck and place her back on the ground to stand on her own. "You're a big girl now, and I need you to be strong to take care of Alicia and your daddy." Those green eyes stared directly into Tara's soul, and then a phone was ringing. Little Tara, in the dream, begins to shake her head, "No! No! NO! Daddy, don't answer the phone!" The phone kept ringing, and Tara was tossing and turning in the bed. The phone keeps ringing, and she finally realizes it's not in her dream. She bolts upright and grabs the phone off the bedside table.

"This is Tara Sanders." Tara barks more than speak. The connection was terrible, full of static.

Tara knew that it had to be either Matthews or Gomez calling with an update. "Tara, it's SFC Matthews. We have found your mom, and she is safe and secure. We are transporting her to Baghdad, and I will call you again once I have a better connection." Before Tara could even choke out a reply, Matthews ended the connection. Tara stood there and stared ahead at the generic wall art that hung across from her on the wall. They had found her mother, and Emily was safe. She didn't even know how to process this information. Her mom had been alive all this time, and they found her. She had never given up hope, always moving forward, holding on to her instincts that her mom had been out there all these years.

Tara sat the phone back on the receiver and a wave of emotions flooded over her. It was like a huge weight had been lifted from her, not just her shoulders but her entire body. She began to sob uncontrollably. She brought her knees up to her chest and rocked back and forth. Her mom was alive. That's all she could keep thinking in her head. Her mom was alive. Her sobs continued as she realized she couldn't even share the news with anyone. She couldn't call her dad, her sister, or even Nick.

Nick. A new wave of emotions and panic ran through Tara. SFC Matthews hadn't said anything about the medical village. Was Nick, Rosie, Doc, and the rest of the staff safe? Had there been any sort of fighting involved with rescuing her mom as they had anticipated? It dawned on her that even though SFC Matthews had called her to inform her that the primary mission of saving her mom was complete, she still had so many questions and concerns. She worked on calming herself down, knowing that staying huddled in a ball crying wasn't going to solve anything.

Once Tara had calmed down enough, she got up and stretched. It occurred to her that she hadn't showered since arriving from Iraq. And then Tara realized that she had access to a REAL shower! What the hell was she waiting for taking a shower? She grabbed her shower bag and headed to her bathroom. She waited for the water to heat up and got in. She stood under the showerhead, letting the hot water run over her head and down her body. She closed her eyes and leaned into the tiled wall. God, it had felt like an eternity since she had last had a proper shower instead of the quick five-minute showers at the medical village. And then she thought about her mother. How long had it been since she had a shower? How long had it been since she had anything that Tara took for granted? She had to face the reality that the brave woman with the fierce green eyes that Tara remembered from her dreams may not be the woman she was getting back. Tara had no clue what her mom had been through for the last fifteen years, but she knew she was ready to be there for her mom. Tara knew that her dad, sister, grandparents, and others would rally to take care of her. They would get the old Emily Sanders back.

Chapter Five

EMILY

"I can't believe this is her. Can you believe this is the female NCO that has been MIA all these years?" Steffens, a Naval nurse, shakes her head as she changes out IV bags. "Shhhhh, Steffens, I know she's sleeping, but she may be able to hear you. Yeah, I get it; it's crazy to think she's been out there for so long. God, can you imagine all the things she has been through?" Pierce, another nurse, works on the other side of the bed, documenting vitals for the patient.

I hear voices and yet again feel as though I can't open my eyes or move my mouth. I begin to panic since I don't recognize either voice. Somewhere I find the strength to start moving my arms. I start thrashing my arms and try to sit up but feel pressure on my chest.

"Woah there, Sgt. Sanders, it's okay! I am Nurse Pierce, and this is Nurse Steffens. We are here to help you. Please, please calm down." I have no choice but to stop. I now feel two sets of arms on me, holding me down. I flicked my eyes open, and it took a few seconds to register what was going on. It seems as though I am in a building; there are lights overhead, and yes, in fact, there are two females, one on each side of me, staring down at me with pity in their eyes.

I try to sit up again, but the one, I think Pierce, shakes her head. "I'm sorry, Sgt. Sanders, but doctor orders. We can't have you sit up yet. You have some pretty nasty injuries that require you to lay flat on your back." Nasty injuries, I think to myself. They probably have no idea how deep some of those wounds and scars even go. Even I don't know for sure, but I remember every strike, every blow, and realize they each left their mark on my body in some way, shape, or form.

I nod my head to let them know I understand. I still cannot speak, but I now realize that this has less to do with my inability to speak and more that I have a breathing tube down my throat. I point to my mouth, and the kind nurses with pity in their eyes confirm what I suspected.

"Yes, Sgt. Sanders, they had to intubate you during the flight here from Baghdad. The pilots and medics stated that you lost consciousness several times during the flight and had difficulty breathing independently. I'm sure when the doctor comes in here shortly, we can see what he thinks about removing the tube." Pierce squeezes my arm lightly, and I nod so she knows that I understand.

I close my eyes again because even having my eyes open and listening to the nurses' talk is exhausting. I hadn't realized how tired I was. It occurs to me that this is the first actual building I have been in since before leaving the US for Iraq all those years ago. God, how many years had it been? I haven't had a way to track time other than how many times I have carried a child. I know I have been pregnant ten times, but it seems like so much longer than that. Has it been closer to twenty years? I try to ignore the tube that I now know is down my throat. Now that I know it's there, I am fighting the urge to gag and claw at my throat.

I must have fallen back to sleep because I hear more muffled voices. As they get closer, I can discern a new voice. Male. I try not to panic, I try so hard, but I begin to get restless again. Please, don't let it be the monster. Please, I seem to have made it so far. Please don't let him take me back there.

I feel pressure on my arms again, and I hear Pierce's familiar voice. "It's okay, Sgt. Sanders, it's me, Pierce, and I have brought with me Doctor Ramone. He is going to take this tube out of your throat now. You have to remain calm and still. You can do that for us, right?" I nod my head and blink, so she knows I will comply. It is a doctor and not my monster. Dr. Ramone has light brown hair and what appears to be dark blue eyes. Nothing like my monster. He smiles at me as he sanitizes and puts his gloves on.

"Hi there, Sgt. Sanders, I know you have been through a lot. I'm going to remove this tube so you can be a little more comfortable. Your throat is going to be a bit sore for a few days. We will get you some warm tea to help soothe it" Dr. Ramone is quick with his work, and before I even realize it, the tube is out, and my entire throat is on fire. I take a deep breath in and whisper out in a raspy voice, "Milk. Can I have milk, please? Instead of tea?" Everyone stops what they are doing and just stares at me. It dawns on me that these are my first words since I wake up and ask for milk. If they didn't already think I was insane, I am sure they will now. "Sure thing Sgt. Sanders, I think we can arrange a nice glass of milk for you." Pierce again, with that pitiful look in her eyes.

I lay there, flat on my back, staring at the ceiling. Even though there is more room in this space than I am used to, I feel claustrophobic. I begin to notice everything touching my skin—the IVs in my arm, the pulse monitor on my finger. I feel the gown I am wearing, and I begin to itch all over. I feel sweat breaking out over my skin, and my breathing picks up. The monitors I am attached to begin to beep quicker, and an alarm began to go off. Pierce comes jogging back in with a cup and a small blue carton of milk in her hands. She quickly puts them down on the counter and rushes over to my side. "Easy there, Sgt. Sanders, please, you are going to make yourself sick." I begin to hyperventilate. There are so many sounds, so many things touching my skin, the lights are so bright. I can't take any of it, but I can't seem to find the words to explain this to the nurse with pity in her eyes. I begin to toss my head back and forth on the pillow. "I. I. I." I am trying to get something out, but I don't know what I am trying to say. "Please, Sgt. Sanders, you have to take a deep breath. I am going to grab your hand, and I want you to focus on my hand and look me in my eyes." Pierce grabs my hand, and I squeeze it so hard. I do as she instructs me to. I stare directly into her dark brown eyes. I get lost in the abyss of her eyes, and then I feel her rubbing her thumb against my hand. She nods her head, "There you go, Sgt. Sanders, focus on my thumb on your hand. Take a deep breath and keep focusing on my thumb." How did she know that was what I had noticed? Again, I do as instructed, and I slowly begin to calm down and find a steady breathing pattern.

"I can't even try to comprehend what you have been through, Sgt. Sanders, but I need you to try your best to remain calm. I promise you are safe. No one can hurt you here." Pierce continues to hold my hand, now bringing her other hand over to enclose my hand between both of her hands. I continue to focus on my breathing, and I don't take my eyes off of her. I lick my lips and muster out a whisper. "Emily. My name is

Emily; you don't have to keep calling me Sgt. Sanders." I force a small smile, which gives Pierce some reassurance that I am calming down.

"Okay, Emily, but if I get in trouble for not following rank, I'm telling the doctor you ordered me to call you by your first name." She squeezed my hand one last time and let go. She raises my upper body in the bed, and I immediately feel a sense of relief. Lying flat on my back was what had started the panic attack. "Thank you, Pierce. I'm not sure what happened just now, but lying flat on my back is not good. It makes me feel like I am trapped again." I have no idea why I felt I had to explain myself to this nurse, but I needed her to know. Pierce nods her head as she walks back over to where she had set down the milk carton.

"As I said, Emily, I have no idea what you have been through, and you do not have to talk about it if you are not ready to. There will be plenty of doctors coming soon enough that will encourage you to share what happened to you. But for now, just know that I am here for you, whether you need more milk or someone to talk to." And with that, she handed me a glass of milk with a straw in it. She grabbed my hand and placed the cup in my palm. I held on with both hands and brought the straw to my lips. I sipped slowly at first and closed my eyes as the cold milk hit my tongue. I closed my eyes to try to stop the tears from coming. But they came anyway. The tears rolled down my cheeks as I sipped on the cold milk. Pierce rubbed my back but didn't say a word. Somehow, she must have known how sacred this moment was. Cold milk is such a simple request, but it means so much to me. I never thought I would drink milk again. I never thought I would be rescued and safe in a secure building.

I finished off the milk and wiped my tears away with my blanket. Pierce handed me a tissue, and I took what she gave me. She took away the empty cup and the used tissue. I looked around the room with fresh eyes. Now that I was sitting up, I felt more secure. "Pierce, do you know if the Army has contacted my family?" Pierce finished cleaning up and was looking at my IV bag when she replied. "I believe the Special Forces team lead has notified your family, but I don't have any details. That is above my paygrade." She smiled at me, and I realized that Nurse Pierce was an exceptional human being.

"That makes sense. Would it be possible to speak with one of the Special Forces team leads then?" I was anxious to see my girls and Josh. God, would the kids even know me? Would I recognize them? I tried not to worry about any of that because first, I needed to understand how they had rescued me. "Let me see if I can find the doctor first. I know he wanted to make sure you were stable before bringing in anyone to speak with you about the series of events that got you here. We need to make sure your body can handle the stress to talk about everything." Pierce gave me one more pat on the arm and then headed over to the door. "I am going to go find Dr. Ramone now. If you need me, punch that red button on the bed next to your right arm." I look down, and sure enough, there is a red stop sign looking button. "You hit that, and I will come back stat." I nod at Pierce, and she walks out of the room. I lean my head back and close my eyes. I focus on the sounds out in the hallway. People are talking about other patients, footsteps on the tiled floor. I remind myself that I am safe and decide that I need to keep repeating that over and over again.

I must have drifted off to sleep because I wake up to hear Nurse Pierce and Dr. Ramone talking as they walk in together. I yawn and rub my eyes open. Dr. Ramone looks down at the chart and makes a few scribbles before looking back over to me. "How was your milk Sgt. Sanders?" I smile at the doctor, wondering if Pierce had told him about the panic attack I had when she brought me the milk. "The milk was heavenly. I forgot how good it was." The doctor nodded and scribbled some more in the chart. He walked towards me, stopping next to the middle of the bed. "May I?" He pointed at my wrist, and I offered him my hand. He took my thin wrist between his fingers and checked my pulse the old fashion way. I found this odd since he could quickly check the machine that was monitoring it constantly. It made me wonder if it was just an old habit from medical school.

Dr. Ramone gently placed my hand back on the bed. His hands were so warm, and it made me realize that even though I had blankets on me and was in a heated building, I was still chilled. I could tell he was getting ready to deliver some sort of news to me, good or bad; I wasn't quite sure. "Sgt. Sanders, I know you asked about your family. We have notified them, and your oldest daughter Tara should be here by tomorrow morning. Your husband and daughter Alicia will be here by the end of the week. They are all extremely anxious to see you. But before we can allow any family visitors, I have to make sure you are up for the visits. I'm sure you are aware of this, but your body is in pretty bad shape. We have done some initial assessments, but we were waiting until you were awake and ready to talk about the extent of your injuries. With that said, I am also recommending we have a therapist come here to speak to you about the traumas you have been through."

I'm not even sure where I begin. Do I begin with the ambush? Or do I begin with being dragged through the streets? Or when the flesh of my legs was falling off with every step my monster took? I nod my head at the doctor, knowing that if I protest speaking to a therapist, it will only delay seeing my family. "I understand, Dr. Ramone. Whatever we have to do to get this moving. I want to be able to see my girls and husband as soon as I can."

Chapter Six

JOSH

Josh hung up the phone, staring out the windows facing the backyard. The call had been with 1LT Gomez, who had finally given Josh more details about Emily. It turns out that Tara had been right all these years. Emily was a prisoner in a village not far from the original ambush site all those years ago. They were still working through details of Emily's imprisonment, but they knew she had been kept on and off in a hole in the ground. Over the years, her captor raped her and forced Emily to bear children. When the Lieutenant had shared this part, Josh had wanted to throw up. God, she had been through so much, but to be raped and then forced to have children took her captivity to an entirely different level of hell.

Josh heard Dina walking in from her day at work. He still hadn't shared anything with her yet about Emily. He had been waiting for the call he had just finished, and now that he had more details, it truly felt real. Not to mention that the Army was already working on booking his and Alicia's flight to Germany. Tara was already on her way there, having been able to fly to Germany faster since she had been in Kuwait and had been the only civilian to know about the mission to rescue her mother.

"Hey there, babe," Dina said as she threw her work bag and purse on the couch. She came up behind Josh and wrapped her arms around his waist. "How was your day? Wait, let me guess. It was amazing because you are retired." She loved teasing him about his retirement and was low-key a little jealous that she still had to work. When he didn't answer her right away and dish back anything, she dropped her hands and waited for him to turn around. After all the years they had been together, she could sense when something wasn't right with him. "What's wrong, Josh? And don't feed me a line of bullshit. You haven't been yourself for a few days now." She stood there in front of him, crossing her arms on her chest. God, she was gorgeous. Her dark black hair framed her face perfectly. He truly loved her, and he knew what he was about to say would break her in half.

Josh took a deep breath and decided it was best to rip the band-aid right off. "Emily is alive. She was found earlier this week and is in a hospital in Germany. Alicia and I are planning to fly out tomorrow morning to be with her. Tara is already there. Tara is the reason they found her. She never gave up on her mom, and now Emily is back." Dina took a step backward, staring at Josh in disbelief. He stayed put, wanting to give her space, knowing that he had just unloaded an atomic bomb on her. After staring at each other for several moments, Dina shook her head up and down and said, "Go. You have to go and bring Emily home." She wasn't looking at Josh any longer, more so staring through him, as if she could already see into the future where there wasn't a place for Dina.

Josh took a step forward, and Dina stayed where she was. He put his arms around her, but she kept her arms wrapped around herself. "Look, Dina, I don't even know how to comprehend all this right now, and I sure as hell don't expect you to either. Please know that I love you, but...." Josh paused, and Dina jumped in with where he was afraid to go. "But you loved Emily first. I know. I remember you working through the grief. You never stopped loving her. I know this." Josh kept his arms wrapped around her, hoping she would reciprocate his embrace, but she kept her arms wound up tight around herself. "I love you, Josh Sanders, and I know you have to do this. I can't stop you from being with your girls and their mother. Go. I will be here when you get back, and I guess we will figure everything out then." Dina pushed herself away from him, turned around, and walked away. Josh stood there, still speechless. He let her walk away and didn't say a word. Josh didn't try to stop her or convince her that she was the love of his life. He couldn't do it because he knew it wasn't true. Josh had allowed himself to fall in love with Dina because the government had told him his wife was dead. He had no choice but to move on, and now here he was over a decade later, and the one true love of his life was alive.

Dina came out of their bedroom with a small overnight bag. "I'm going to stay at my sister's tonight. Let me know when you make it to Germany, okay?" Josh nodded, and Dina walked out to the garage. As quickly as he had dropped the bomb of Emily being alive on Dina, it was as quickly as she was now gone. He couldn't help but feel as though they both knew where his loyalties would lie. His phone began to buzz in his hands. It was his younger daughter Alicia. Thank goodness she had arrived back in the states from her missionary trip. He took the call and braced himself for another rip-off the band-aid moment. The call was brief since, as soon as he told her the news of her mother, she said she was on her way over and hung up. That was how it always went with her. She was hot-headed and to the point like him. She didn't want details over the phone, plus as much as he didn't want to admit it, he needed her here with him right now. He still had to call Emily's mom since the Army only called the next of kin, which was Josh. It was his responsibility to tell and retell the story of Emily's rescue to the family.

While Josh waited for Alicia to arrive, he called Rodriguez back and told him he should head over too. Since Dina was gone for the night, he might as well make this Emily HQ. Josh went to his bedroom and grabbed a backpack from the closet, and began stuffing clothes into it, not thinking about what he was packing or what he would need. He had no idea how long they would be in Germany, but he knew he could always find a PX store on base if he needed anything.

"Dad!!" Josh could hear Alicia yelling from the front hall. Somehow, he hadn't even heard her pull in or the front door open. He must have been deep in his head while he was packing. "I'm in the bedroom." He hollered back at her. Alicia stopped in the doorway, the second spitting image of Emily, with Tara being the first one. They both just stood there staring at each other, and then Alicia, with her dark green eyes, choked up a cry or a moan, Josh couldn't tell, and she ran into his arms. "Daddy, she's alive?!" He held on to her just as tight as she held on to him. Even though she had been a baby when Emily had gone missing, she grew up hearing all the stories about her mom from Tara, Rodriguez, and the rest of their family. He had no idea how she was processing this right now. It dawned on him that they all were processing it differently. But for Alicia, this was like the ghost of Christmas past was back for good. He cleared his throat, realizing he had never answered the question she had just posed at him. "Yeah, sweetie, your mom is alive. I have some details but not many. I just know that Tara is already on her way to Germany to see her. She always said she felt her mom was still alive and she wouldn't give up on her. And she was right. Dammit, she was right." Josh could feel Alicia crying, and he held her tighter. They stood there like that for who knows how long. The next thing Josh knew, he heard the front door opening up again. Rodriguez. He had already forgotten that he had invited him over.

Josh pulled away from Alicia and went out to the living room. Alicia followed him, and when Alicia saw Rodriguez, she ran to him and brought him in for a tight embrace as well. "Roddie, my mom is alive! She's alive, and Tara found her!" Rodriguez hugged her back, staring over her shoulder at Josh. "That's why I'm here. That's why I'm here." After everyone had shed more tears, the three went into the living room, Alicia and Rodriguez sitting down while Josh stayed standing. He was too anxious to sit, and he needed to pace while he shared what details he had with the two of them.

Josh shared everything he knew from his conversation with 1LT Gomez. He didn't hold back anything, even the parts he had learned about the rapes and children. They all needed to fully understand what Emily had been through if they were going to help her. Alicia sat on the couch with her legs brought up to her chest, silent tears falling from her cheeks. Rodriguez stared ahead in a daze. Josh was confident he was back in Iraq in his head, reliving every action that led to leaving Emily and Grant behind. He would feel the guilt of what Emily had been through the most, and Josh didn't know how to help him out of that dark place.

They all agreed that Josh needed to call Emily's mom. With Josh and Alicia leaving in the morning, he couldn't waste any more time. Josh came and sat between Alicia and Rodriguez and made the call. Just as Josh was getting ready to hit send on the phone, he realized that Emily didn't know her dad had passed away. God, it had only been a few years, and even Josh forgot from time to time. Just a minute ago, he thought he would call and talk to both her mom and dad. Josh added that to his mental checklist of obstacles they would have to climb over when the time came. He hit send, and Emily's mom, Evelyn Moore, answered on the second ring. "Hi Josh, my long-lost prodigal son." Josh smiled a little. Evelyn still referred to him as her son since Emily had been their only child. He tried to stay in touch with her, but sometimes it was too hard to talk to her when she typically only wanted to talk about Emily. Before Josh could hang up or hand the phone to Alicia, he said calmly, "Evelyn, I need you to sit down. Can you do that for me?" He heard her shuffle, and then he could tell she was sitting down. "Okay, honey, I'm sitting. Is everything okay? Are the girls okay?" He could hear the panic in her voice, but he needed to make sure she was sitting because he wasn't sure her heart could take this. He wished he could deliver this news in person, but there just wasn't enough time to fly to Ohio before heading to Germany tomorrow.

"Yes, the girls are fine. Alicia is right here with me, and Tara is on her way to Germany." He looked at Alicia, and she nudged him as if to say, get on with it already! "Germany? What is she going there for? I thought her volunteer trip was in Iraq or Kuwait?" Evelyn could never keep the countries in the Middle East straight, and Josh had wondered if Evelyn did this on purpose. "No, she was in Iraq for her volunteer trip, but plans changed. She, um." Josh paused and looked from Alicia to Rodriguez. All of a sudden, all the emotions flooded over him, and he had to take a deep breath to get the following sentence out. "Tara is going to Germany because she found Emily. Emily is alive."

There was complete silence on the other end, and Josh wasn't sure if Evelyn had passed out or not. "Evelyn, are you there? Please say something, so I know you are okay." He heard a deep gasp in and then a long sigh. "Oh Josh, are you sure? Are you certain it's Emily?" The pain in her voice was unbearable to him. This was why he had waited until he had some details before calling her. Because they had been down this road before, chasing sightings, rumors in villages, but they always turned up a dead end. Josh closed his eyes and gripped the phone tighter. "Yes, they have a positive ID on Emily. One of Tara's friends had identified Emily. When the volunteer had rolled up Emily's sleeve, she noticed a faded tattoo that was the same one Tara had. The volunteer knew Tara's background, and her passion for being there in Iraq was more than just to help children get their vaccinations. When the volunteer saw the tattoo, she didn't say anything to Emily in fear of drawing attention to the situation. She later told Tara, who then went to their head doctor. From there, they connected with the Special Forces team that has had boots on the ground for some time now still doing surveillance on some other potential security risks. After several more weeks of surveillance on Emily's village, the Special Forces team took the strike. I don't have all the details of the rescue, but from what it sounds like, Emily was in pretty rough shape when they found her. Alicia and I are flying to Germany tomorrow to be with her and Tara." Josh took a deep breath and waited for the onslaught of questions to come. But there was only silence on the other end.

Then Josh could hear her sniffling, and he knew she was crying.

"I want to see her. Can I go with you and Alicia tomorrow?" Evelyn's voice cracked, and she sounded every bit of seventy-five years old. Josh closed his eyes, not wanting to say the next part. "I'm sorry, Evelyn, but only next of kin can see her right now. She has been through many traumas, and they aren't sure how much she will be able to handle. I promise you, as soon as we can skype with Emily, we will do so. And you will be the first person she sees when she is stateside."

More crying, God, Josh hated doing this to his mother-in-law. He should have been there in person, holding her hands. But instead, they were hundreds of miles apart, and she was all alone. Another person left to cope with Emily's rescue on their terms. After more reassurance that he would call Evelyn as soon as he landed, he hung up the phone and leaned back against the couch. Alicia leaned over and laid her head on his chest like she used to do when she was little. Josh's emotional tank was running on empty, and he knew that this journey had just begun. For so many years, Josh had prayed for this moment. He had yearned to know that Emily was alive and would be home with their girls. But all the praying and yearning had turned to a sense of being forsaken. He had picked up the broken pieces of his small family and had done the best he could to move on. Here they all were, broken open once again. With all the emotions flooding in at once like a dam had just been broken open, and the waters were rushing in uncontrollably.

Chapter Seven

EMILY

2019. That was what year it is. Fifteen years since I had last seen my daughters or husband. One of the nurses had removed all the tubes and IV bags, and I could lay on my left side, which was my good side. I lay like this now, staring at the wall, thinking about the year. 2019. I had been gone for over a decade. Dr. Ramone had a counselor slash therapist come into work with me for a few hours every day. As if telling me what year we were in wasn't enough, she had also informed me that my family had buried an empty casket. The Army had declared me a KIA- killed in action after eight years of not being found. So that would mean that in 2012 when I had already been raped more than five times and had given birth to five children, the United States Army had declared me dead. That was when I sent the kind counselor, who they called CeeCee away. I couldn't handle any more information for the day.

I had been in Germany for several days and had been through more tests, scans, and meetings than I could take. They had determined that most of my injuries were healed, not healed in the best way, but healed. Dr. Ramone and his team stated that while I was in their care, the focus would be on regaining my strength, which started with building up my weight and nutrition. Once I was strong enough to fly back to the states, I would spend time at Walter Reed Hospital in Maryland, going through physical therapy and more counseling sessions than I wanted to consider.

I noticed there was a small crack in the wall. It was probably structural, and it reminded me of the wall in the hut back in Iraq. At night, I would stare at it, thinking about how I felt so much like the crack in a wall. Slowly, over time, spreading and breaking off into other cracks before finally becoming too big for any sort of repair. For the first time since being in Germany, I thought about the children. I wondered what would become of them. Indeed, they would be placed in some sort of foster care or go up for adoption. As much as I wanted to love them, I wasn't sure if I could ever look at them without feeling absolute hatred for the monster. But then I think about the crystal the older children had given me and how baby Asad would hold on to my finger when I nursed him. Was it the children's fault for having to live this life?

I heard a knock on my door, which must have become standard protocol for all staff coming in to check on me. Since I had been relatively calm and complacent, the medical staff were all taking that to mean I was still in a dark place. "Come in," I said in a flat tone, not having the energy to roll over to see who it was. "Sgt. Sanders," Oh okay, so this was someone new to the team. I instructed the regular staff to call me Emily. No need to keep the formalities going any longer. According to the Army, I wasn't even alive right now, let alone a sergeant in their Army. "You can call me Emily; I am sure it's in the charts." I heard a male voice clear his throat, which caught my attention since the person who said my name did not have a deep baritone. I rolled over to see Nurse Pierce with two tall Army soldiers looming in the doorway behind her. I sat up and brushed back my hair as if that would help me look any more professional.

"Sgt. Sanders, this is 1LT Gomez and SFC Matthews. They were the team leads on your rescue operation. They were hoping to talk to you for a few minutes." Nurse Pierce, who had become more than just my nurse, came over and did a quick check of my pulse and tucked in the blankets around my waist. "Do you need anything before I leave you three to talk?" I smiled at her and realized how genuinely kind she was. She went above and beyond her standard nurse duties, and I added her to my list of people I probably would never be able to repay with gratitude. "No, thank you, Pierce. I am good to go." With that, Pierce walked out behind the two soldiers and closed the door for privacy.

"Sgt. Sanders, on behalf of our Special Forces team and the United States Army, we want to extend our gratitude to you for your service to our country. And I'm sure I speak for SFC Matthews as well when I say how great it is to see you in your current state." 1LT Gomez looked over to SFC Matthews, and I could tell that even though Gomez was the officer in charge, he looked to Matthews for support and reassurance. Matthews, tall and lean, had a stern face. He looked to be probably in his early thirties, and she wondered if Josh knew him. "I hadn't known I looked that bad when you found me." As soon as the words left my mouth, I remembered I was speaking to an officer, and even though I didn't feel like I was in the Army anymore, I knew to these guys, the military protocol was everything. "Sorry, sir, I didn't mean to be so frank. It's just nice to speak to the military rather than medical staff finally. I think if I hear about my injuries one more time and how lucky I am to be alive, I may crawl out of my skin."

I motion with my hands to the chairs next to the bed for them to sit down. "Please sit; having you both standing at parade rest is making me have the urge to do the same, and unfortunately, I don't think I would be up to military standards." They followed my recommendation, and they both sat down almost in unison. "I guess it's my turn to thank you both for rescuing me. I have my suspicions as to how you found me, but I hope you can share with me at least some of the details. I understand if I cannot know all the details of the operation."

Again, 1LT Gomez looks to SFC Matthews, and Matthews nods to Gomez to signal him to begin. "Sgt. Sanders, you have two daughters, who are both alive and well. Tara has spent the last six months in Iraq, volunteering with a non-profit organization to administer vaccinations to the locals. She volunteered for this mission under the pretense that you were still alive. She's a resilient young woman quite frankly and has spent most of her life and education bringing herself to Iraq." He paused there as if to give me time to ask questions, but I wanted to hear everything he had to say before distracting him from his train of thought. When I didn't say anything, he continued.

"She originally only confided in two fellow volunteers. Her fiancé, Nick, and her friend Rosita." When he said Rosita's name, it all came back to me. The day at the clinic. Rosita rolled up my sleeve and casually saw my faded tattoo but did not bring any attention to it. She had known. So, when I saw her raise her arm in a fist to me as we walked away, that was her way of telling me she knew. I thought I had made it all up in my head. That same night when we had arrived back to our village, I was thrown back into my hole and had completely lost track of time, and memories had begun to fade quickly.

The Lieutenant continued, "Do you remember the day you came to the medical village Sgt. Sanders?" I nodded and cleared my throat as it had become parched. I reached over from the bedside table and grabbed my glass of water. After a few sips, I felt like I could respond. "Yes, I remember that day. I had been shocked I was allowed to leave my hut. It was my first trip outside of where I lived all these years. The oldest boys explained to me that their father wanted me to receive the shots like the children so I could safely continue having more children for him." I stopped there, not ready to go into all the details of what 'having children' when you were a prisoner meant. I was surprised they had not had me give an official statement yet on what had happened to me all those years ago, but I knew it was coming soon.

1LT Gomez nodded and looked down at his hands in his lap. "When Rosita was working with your family, she was able to identify you. Lucky for you and us, she remained calm. Had she acted suspiciously or out of the ordinary, we are confident it would have alerted the older boys that something was up." At the mention of Mahir and Maimun, I sat up a little straighter. I promised myself not to interrupt, but I couldn't help myself. "Mahir and Maimun. Where are they now?" I could tell he was not ready for this question. He looked at me and with an even composure and said, "They escaped with their father. When we infiltrated the village, they took the defense with Mohammad. We have been following Mohammad for some time now. We had several leads from other sources that Mohammad was preparing a new round of insurgence in Northern Iraq. We did additional recon and confirmed our suspicions."

I took another sip of water and leaned back against my pillows. I was utterly exhausted, and even though I wanted to hear more, I couldn't go on any longer. "I'm sorry, sir, but can we finish this conversation later? I need to rest." I kept my eyes closed to signal to them that I did not want to continue this discussion. It was just too much, the rescue, the hospital, the talking to everyone about all the things. I didn't know how I was going to get through this. "We completely understand Sgt. Sanders." This time it was a different male voice, and I realized SFC Matthews hadn't spoken up to this point. "Although we will never truly understand the hell you have been through, trust me, we understand the not wanting to continue talking. Try to get some rest. We don't know if the staff has told you yet, but Tara is on her way here to see you. She will arrive tomorrow, and within the next day or so, MSG Sanders and Alicia should be arriving." I kept my eyes closed even though hearing my kids' names did make my heart rate increase. I heard them both stand up and walked out of the room. I rolled back over to my left side and took up my staring at the crack-in-the-wall routine. Tara was coming to see me. Alicia and Josh were coming to see me. There are so many emotions to feel right now, but yet I feel numb inside.

Chapter Eight

TARA

Tara tapped her foot relentlessly as she waited in the lobby of the hotel in Kuwait. SFC Matthews had contacted her and told her to be ready in the lobby at 0600 hours. He was already in Germany with the rest of the Special Forces Team that had been with her mom, but he had additional soldiers coming to pick her up and take her to Camp Doha to fly out to Landstuhl. She looked up and saw a Humvee pull up, and she knew this was her ride. She stood and headed to the front entrance. A female soldier got out of the driver's seat and met Tara at the doors. "Ma'am, I am SSG Lewis. To confirm, you are Tara Sanders?" The sergeant had dark brown eyes and a kind smile. Tara didn't let that deceive her, though. If SSG Lewis was under SFC Matthews command, that meant she was a bon-a-fide badass. Now accepted females could test their endurance and go through the rigors of Special Forces training. Tara knew that SSG Lewis was well trained and would protect Tara if it came down to it.

Tara nodded and smiled back at SSG Lewis, "Yes, Sergeant, I am Tara Sanders." SSG Lewis nodded back to the lobby, "Are you ready to go, or do you need to check out still?" "Nope, I took care of all that already. I'm good to go." Tara would probably have run to Germany if she had to. She hadn't slept well because of the levels of adrenaline running through her veins. Tara was going to be with her mother. The woman that she had spent her entire life searching for and preparing for this moment.

Tara followed SSG Lewis to the Humvee, threw her two bags in the back, and hopped in. The ride to Camp Doha felt like it took an eternity. Traffic was terrible in Kuwait City, and the camp was about 45 minutes away on a good day of traffic. Tara put her earbuds in and decided to listen to some music to help calm her nerves. Now that she had been in Kuwait, her cell service worked, although she still had not had contact with her family, per orders from SFC Matthews and 1LT Gomez. She scrolled through her music library and landed on Pearl Jam. Her mom had loved Pearl Jam and teased her dad that Eddie Vedder was her future husband if things didn't pan out with him. Tara always knew her mom was teasing when she would flash her smile at her dad. Would her mom still have that gorgeous smile? The smile that could melt your heart and make you smile no matter how bad your mood.

State of Love and Trust came on, and Tara closed her eyes and let herself be swept away by the song. Before she knew it, they were going through a series of stops and go, which meant they must be entering the base. She opened her eyes, and sure enough, they were coming through the final checkpoint and entering Camp Doha. They kept driving and made their way to the tarmac, where various military aircraft were at different stages of either just landing or preparing for takeoff. The Humvee pulled over to a set of hangars and parked in the shade. Even though it was only close to 0700 in the morning, the sun was already getting hot in the sky. They got out of the

Humvee, and SSG Lewis left Tara and the driver behind to speak with what appeared to be their pilot. Tara got her bags out of the back and grabbed her water bottle, knowing she needed to stay hydrated and strong for her mom.

SSG Lewis walked back over to Tara and explained they would be flying out on an Airbus A400M Atlas, not the most comfortable flight, but it would get the job done. Since there was a limited amount of military personnel involved, the Special Forces team was working with what was available. Outside of senior leadership in the Army, no one had a clue what had happened and, for that matter, that the country's first-ever presumed dead soldier was indeed alive. Tara followed SSG Lewis to the aircraft and walked in through the tail end. Since this was nothing like a typical airplane, the seats were lined up against the plane's walls, with plenty of space in the middle of the aircraft to fit entire tanks if needed. This explained why they were able to catch a ride back to Germany. This particular aircraft made rounds from Germany to Kuwait regularly on supply runs and was headed back to Landstuhl with broken down Humvees for repair at the base in Germany where there were more resources available.

Tara secured her bags and got herself strapped into the harness in her seat. SSG Lewis sat two seats away from her on her right. The engines came to life as the plane began to warm up. SSG Lewis signaled to Tara. "Here! Take these and keep them in so you don't blow an ear drum. The flight should be a pretty smooth ride, and it's only about five and half hours to Germany. Try to get a nap in if you can." With that, SSG Lewis handed Tara a small foil-sealed pack of earplugs. As the engines began to warm up, she understood why Lewis had given them to her. The roar of the engines was deafening. She stuck them in her ears and took a deep breath. They began to taxi onto the airstrip, and she tried to remain calm, but all she could think about was how she would see her mom in just a few hours.

Surprisingly to Tara, she had fallen asleep on the flight. She woke up to the jolt of the landing gears hitting the ground and the aircraft slowing down. Tara waited for the signal from SSG Lewis to unbuckle and take her ear plugs out. They remained in their seats until all the equipment was removed, and then they walked out the backend of the aircraft. Germany was two hours behind Kuwait in time. Tara updated her phone when they landed to see that it was only approaching noon, Germany time. She continued to follow SSG Lewis to a group of Army officers and higher-ranking NCOs standing by several black SUVs, she assumed for them.

SSG Lewis saluted and then shook hands with what appeared to be a Colonel and a Sergeant Major. Tara was grateful that her dad taught her and Alicia the rank structure of the Army and all the military branches. SSG Lewis turned back around to Tara. "Well, Tara, this is where we part ways. It has been an honor to bring you to Germany to see your mother finally. I pray you and your family will finally have the peace you have been searching for." And with that, SSG Lewis reached out her palm, and Tara shook her hand. It was surreal to think so many people had invested not only their time but also risked their lives to save her mother, and they didn't even know her. But that didn't matter, and that was what had always amazed Tara about the military. The camaraderie, the bonds they all shared no matter if they knew you or not. It was one big family.

The group of distinguished leaders introduced themselves to Tara. Most of them were the leaders in charge of the base in Landstuhl. Of course, they would all want to meet her, the daughter of the long-lost soldier. They stood there for a moment, telling her how proud they were of her for not giving up on her mother and how amazing it must feel to know her mom was alive. Tara felt like they were all stalling her, holding her off because they had to deliver some bad news or something.

Out of the corner of her eye, she saw two more men in uniform walking towards the group. Right away, she recognized them, and immediately her heart leaped in her chest. 1LT Gomez and SFC Matthews walked up and smiled huge grins at Tara. Before Tara could stop herself, she ran over and hugged first 1LT Gomez and then SFC Matthews. These two men were the real reason her mom was here, and Tara would be eternally grateful to them both. SFC Matthews pulled back from her hug, and she could tell he was a bit emotional by the glaze on his eyes. "I don't think there are enough words in the dictionary for me to tell you both how thankful I am for you saving my mom, but also that you and your teams are safe." Now Tara could feel herself beginning to choke up, and she didn't even care how much brass was watching them. SFC Matthews nodded his head and spoke. "Tara, you are the true hero here. Without your perseverance to find your mom, we would not have known she was still alive. We did what we were trained to do. So, thank you for your fierce tenacity."

1LT Gomez cleared his throat, "I hate to break up our time here, but I think there is someone you have been waiting to see for a very long time. We are going to ride with you over to the hospital and get you up to speed on your mom's condition." Tara nodded, excited but also nervous and scared. She had no clue what kind of condition her mom might be in, but she knew it couldn't be good. The three of them jumped into one of the SUVs parked along the airstrip. Once they were inside, 1LT Gomez, who had taken the passenger seat while SFC Matthews drove, turned around so he could look at Tara when talking to her.

"Tara, I'm sure you are aware, but I need to prep you for what you are going to see when you meet your mother. It's been a long time since you last saw her, and it can be shocking sometimes initially. Please know that we have a counselor on standby for you and your family once they arrive. Your mom does remember you, your sister, and your dad. She is aware of what year it is and that the actual combat operations are over in Iraq. She has been through many traumas, and I'm not sure what she will want to share with you or your family. When we get to the hospital, I believe Dr. Ramone will meet with you before entering your mother's room. You will need to be prepared for the physical condition too. Even though she is 45 years old, she looks a lot older. Her aging is normal, considering how long she was kept captive and the amount of malnutrition she has endured. You have to do your best to remain calm and not let her see you get upset by her appearance." He paused and looked at SFC Matthews in the driver's seat. Matthews nodded at Gomez to continue as if the lieutenant needed the reassurance from the more seasoned NCO. Tara had a feeling there was a lot they were not telling her, and she had a feeling that it may have to do with the children.

"What about her children?" Tara asked the question so abruptly, 1LT Gomez was not ready for it. "The children. I know she has children. That is how I figured this all out. I also determined that she did not have all those children of her own free will. So please, do not feel like you have to hide or sugar coat anything for me. She is my mother, and if I am going to help her recover, I need to know everything." Tara waited for Gomez to continue. He nodded his head up and down.

"Yes, you are correct; she had children. She has eight children. We rescued six of them from the village. But their father and the oldest two boys fled. We are still following leads, and since their father was her captor, we are now preparing for an additional operation to secure all three of them." Tara tried to swallow but felt like her throat was full of sand. Mahir and Maimun. They were with their father. And the other six children were here? What was she supposed to do with them? She found her voice again and asked another pointed question. "You brought the children to Germany. Who is going to take care of them?" Gomez looked at Matthews, and even though Gomez was the officer in charge, she could tell that he leaned on Matthews quite a bit since he had served longer. "Well, that is still being determined. They are with a social worker, and the medical staff will medically and mentally evaluate them. Technically speaking, they are your mother's children. If I had to guess, they are going to be with your mother." Tara couldn't even try to comprehend what this would mean not only for her mother but for Tara and the rest of them. She hadn't even considered what would happen to the children. And quite frankly, she didn't care. In her mind, the Special Forces team was sent in to rescue her mother, so Tara, her dad, and Alicia could take her home and live happily ever after. Now there was another whole level of complications.

"Look, Tara, if I am honest with you, rescuing your mother was probably the easiest part of all this. No one in the military has dealt with a case like this in a very long time. Your mother was in captivity for close to fifteen years. The trauma she endured is just one hurdle you will have to help her overcome. Think about all the technological advancements you have witnessed growing up. iPhones, Google, Netflix, Amazon, these are just a few things that your mother doesn't even know about yet. She will have a ton of adjusting and coping with what to do with these kids. I am only telling you all this because you have to prepare yourself before walking into her room for the first time. Neither I nor SFC Matthews is a doctor or expert when it comes to the brain, but we can tell you that you are going to have to have a lot of patience going forward." 1LT Gomez stopped there and turned back around in his seat. She had been so deep in conversation with him that she hadn't even noticed that they had arrived at the hospital. SFC Matthews parked the SUV in a spot assigned for active-duty personnel, and they got out. She grabbed her bags because she had no idea if Gomez and Matthews would be here later. And actually, Tara had no idea where she was staying while she was here. She would sleep in a chair next to her mom's bed if it were up to her.

As the three of them walked up the main steps into the hospital, Tara felt like she was going to throw up right then and there. She swallowed it down and told herself to get it together. She followed SFC Matthews and 1LT Gomez through the maze of the hospital. They were all silent, Matthews and Gomez periodically scanning the halls, and Tara knew that was natural for them. Her dad was the same way, constantly checking a room, securing it in his mind, and knowing the way out, just in case something terrible happened. They took an elevator up to the intensive care unit. Nausea in her stomach got stronger, and she tried to inhale and exhale through her nose to keep herself calm. When they got off the elevator, they took a few more turns down hallways before stopping in front of an office door with the name Dr. J. Ramone on the nameplate. 1LT Gomez knocked once, and a male's voice on the other side told them to come in.

When Tara and the Special Forces leaders walked into the office, a middle-aged doctor with light brown hair and dark blue eyes stood to greet them. Dr. Ramone was on the ID badge hanging from his white jacket pocket. He stood up and walked around the desk to stand right in front of Tara, completely bypassing Matthews and Gomez. "I presume you are Tara?" The doctor asked her. Tara nodded and cleared her throat. "Yes, I am Tara Sanders." The doctor smiled and stuck out his hand, "Well, I am Dr. Ramone, and it is a true honor to meet you." They shook hands, and Dr. Ramone guided her to sit down while Matthews and Gomez remained standing near the closed door. Dr. Ramone walked back around the desk and took a seat. His demeanor reminds her so much of Doc back at the medical village in Iraq, and for a quick moment, she wondered if she would have this same demeanor with families and patients one day.

Dr. Ramone opened up a folder on his desk and began pulling out paperwork and a photo. "Tara, I know you are aware that your mother is here. We have been able to ID her, but I do have some photos of her that I would like to show you." He started to pass them across his desk but then pulled them back at the last moment. "I should add that the woman in these photos may not resemble the woman you remember or what she looked like in the photos you may have of her." Tara nodded, unable to find words to speak. He handed her the photos, and she took them gently from his hands. Tara stared at the first photo and had to blink several times to stop the tears from falling. The woman staring back at her was indeed her mother, but at the same time was a different person.

She could tell by the eyes staring back at her that it was Emily. But the scars and disfiguration of her nose were proof that her mother had been to hell and back. She moved on to the next photo, which was simply a picture of her mom's tattoo on her wrist, the same one that Tara had on her right forearm. Emily's tattoo was more faded, and there were scars on top of the words Always Forward. They looked like scratches, or maybe they had been lashings. She closed her eyes, trying not to think about what kind of torture her mom had undergone. The last picture was another shot of her mother, but from the side and standing up. From Emily's military files, she had been five foot six before she left for Iraq. This photo looked like a seventy-year-old woman, hunched back from years of osteoporosis setting in. God, her mom wasn't even fifty yet. She handed the photos back to Dr. Ramone, maintaining her composure, even though on the inside she was screaming.

Dr. Ramone began speaking again, and Tara did her best to hear him, nodding when it seemed appropriate. Occasionally, she would listen to him say things like, 'we have a counselor on-site for you and your family,' and 'this will be a long road of recovery for Emily.' And last but not least, 'you have to be patient with her, she may not want to talk about it, and she may not have maternal feelings towards you and your sister.' Tara finally, anxious to see her mother, interrupted Dr. Ramone. "Thank you, Dr. Ramone, for everything. I am sure we will be fine, and we understand this will not be easy. When can I meet my mother?"

Chapter Nine

EMILY

I must have drifted off to sleep because the next thing I know, I smell eggs and bacon in the air and roll over away from my cracked wall that had become my home. Nurse Pierce was beginning to walk out when she heard me shifting in bed. "Hey there, Emily, good morning!" She was always in a good mood, but she appeared to be in even better spirits this morning. "Wow, you are just a bundle of joy today, Nurse Pierce," I say as I sit up and pull the rolling bedside table closer to me. It occurs to me that I must have slept through dinner last night. My stomach lets out a loud growl to confirm the missed meal.

"Well, once I tell you who is coming today, I think you will be just as excited." Pierce turns her back and begins pulling items out of a cabinet. I start shoveling scrambled eggs into my mouth, still working on my coordination skills with utensils. "Okay, spill it. Who do I have the luxury of spending time with today?" I realize I sound very sarcastic, but I can't believe she would think I would be excited to see more doctors or military personnel after the last few days. She turns back around and sits on the edge of my bed with a stack full of fresh scrubs for me.

Since I no longer was hooked up to monitors, they had allowed me to wear full scrubs instead of the standard hospital gown. "Emily, today is the day Tara arrives. She should be arriving here in Germany in a few hours, and then she will come directly here. You are going to see your daughter! Isn't that exciting?" I picked up a piece of bacon and stared at it. I know what response I should give her. I know I should verbally express how excited I am to see Tara. But I'm not sure excited is the right word. I'm terrified. The last time I saw my daughter, she was barely four years old. What if I didn't know how to act with her? Or worse, what if I didn't feel anything when she walked through the door? "Emily? Are you in there? I said you need to hurry up and finish your breakfast so I can help you into the shower. I want to make sure you are spiffy clean for Tara's arrival." I snapped out of my staring match with the bacon and looked up at Pierce as I shoved the entire strip into my mouth. I nodded my head to let her know I had heard her and finished my breakfast.

After my shower, Pierce helped me back into bed. Even though I was gaining weight, I was still pretty weak and would need a cane at the very least for the rest of my life. I still struggled with bathing, so Pierce stayed in the bathroom with me. Once I was back in bed, Pierce came to the side of the bed and helped me brush my hair. For years, my hair had remained in a braid and only recently washed. Even with that recent washing, it was still gritty and course with dirt. I had already told myself that once I was stateside, I was cutting it all off. It reminded me too much of that life, and I needed it all gone. But for now, Pierce brushed through the golden and greying locks, which looked more platinum than blonde. She then braided it down my back again per my request. Once she finished, I laid my head back on the pillow.

Even just the simplest tasks of showering and getting dressed left me exhausted. "Okay, Emily, you have about an hour or so to catch a quick nap. But just so you know, the next time anyone comes in here, it's going to be with Tara." She patted my leg as she brought my blankets up to my chest. She had learned my signals of when I was ready to shut down. I nodded, too exhausted to even say anything in response.

I hear hushed voices outside my hospital room. I am still in the hospital, right? The lights had gone out from no movement, and the privacy curtains were still in place. I open my eyes and look around. Yes, I am still in the hospital, and I am safe. I am not in Iraq. I raise myself in the bed and smooth out my blankets. I hear the voices and try to decipher what they are saying, but it's useless. The hearing specialist had already told me I only had about twenty percent hearing in each ear, and he had already ordered the hearing aids that I would need for the rest of my life. The next thing I know, the doorknob is twisting, and my heartbeat begins to quicken. The same two men from yesterday walked in first. Was it Gomez and Matthews? I think so, but I can't remember their rank. Behind them, a young woman, roughly around five-seven, walks in. I can't stop staring at her. It's like I am looking at a younger version of myself, from her golden blonde hair, which is up in an unruly bun, to her tan skin and those green eyes.

I feel the tears begin to well up in my eyes. I can tell Tara is nervous about coming in, and she hesitates before looking over at me. I swallow and try to get rid of the dryness in my mouth. I muster out a greeting. "Tara. Oh, Tara, it's so good to see you." If I had been worried, I wouldn't have felt any emotions when I saw my firstborn; those worries were gone at that moment. I sat up more and wanted to get up, but I knew my limitations. She wiped back tears with her hand and came towards the bed.

I opened up my arms, and she collapsed onto the bed, right into my arms. I'm not sure who's tears were who's. We cried and cried for what seemed like hours. After some time, we both pulled away to look at each other. I reached up to tuck a strand of hair that had fallen from her bun behind her ear. "Oh God, Tara, you are so beautiful. I never thought I would see you again." Tara took my hand and squeezed it within her own, and then kissed the back of my hand. "Mama, I never stopped believing in you. I knew I would find you, one way or another." And this time, she brought me in for the embrace, and I laid my head on her chest. It was like our roles reversed, and she was my protector. I heard someone clear their throat, and I realized that Gomez and Matthews must still be in the room with us.

I pulled away from Tara, but she kept a grip on my hands. I sat back a little, the exertion of seeing Tara for the first time in so long having hit me like a brick. But there was no way I was sending her away. Not any time soon. Gomez, ah yes, now I see his rank is the First Lieutenant. He pinches the bridge of his nose and gains his composure. "Sgt. Sanders, we know you and Tara have a lot of catching up to do. And we fully plan on giving you all the time you need, but we will need to come back in a little bit to finish our discussion from yesterday. As well as the higher chain of command from the Pentagon is here. They want to have an after-action review on what has happened to you." I look from Gomez to Matthews, then to my daughter. "They want me to lead an AAR? Like what, this was a training exercise gone bad?" As soon as the words left my mouth, I knew it was inappropriate, but I just got my daughter back, and now they wanted me to relive every godforsaken moment of the last fifteen years? "Look, sir, with all due respect, I just got my daughter back, and I haven't seen my husband or my sweet baby Alicia yet. And not to mention, the Army proclaimed me dead. So, how's that for your AAR?" Screw it; I didn't even care anymore. What were they going to do, give me an Article Fifteen for disrespecting an officer? SFC Matthews stepped up and took over, clearly seeing that Gomez's approach had not been a wise one. "Okay, Sgt. Sanders, how about this? We will come back once you have had time with Tara, Josh, and Alicia? We can hold off the brass for another day or two, but you know this has to happen. If you want to be released to the states, we have to document your story." I looked at Tara and saw my reflection in her eyes. I nodded my head in agreement, and both men left.

Once we are alone, I squeeze Tara's hands, and I can't help but smile. "I can't stop staring at you. I'm sorry if that creeps you out, but it's so hard to believe that you are all grown up. In my head, you have been this sweet little girl, barely able to hold my entire hand. And now here you are, a woman. A strong, courageous woman." Tara looks down, trying to hold back more tears. I continued talking, "Thank you, Tara. Thank you for not giving up on me. Even though as soon as I am strong enough, I may kick your butt for risking your own life in the process." With that, we both laughed, and I began to cough from a sharp pain in my side. Tara stopped and leaned forward.

"Are you okay? Should I call for the nurse?" I shook my head, letting go of her hands so I could take a drink of water. Once I got the coughing under control, I explained. "No, I am fine. I think that might have been my first laugh since being captured. It just woke up muscles in my sides I forgot I had." She rubbed my arm and then reached for my right hand. She turned my wrist over, so my faded tattoo was facing up. She then turned her right wrist so that both our forearms were facing the same way. "Always Forward, I never forgot your motto after all these years, Mom. The tattoo is how Rosie was certain it was you that day at the medical village." She traced the lettering on my arm. I couldn't look up at her because I could feel the tears welling up in my eyes. I cleared my throat, "I know I said this already, but thank you, Tara. You never gave up on me, even when I had given up on myself." She squeezed my hand again, and I laid my head on her shoulder. I left behind a sweet little girl, and in her place was this strong woman, who I now needed to lean on.

"Why don't you lay back, Mom. We have plenty of time to talk. I promise I'm not going anywhere." Tara helps me lay back on the bed and pulls the blankets up to my chest. She's right, the excitement and adrenaline of meeting her are wearing off, and I am all of a sudden exhausted. She takes the seat next to the bed and brings it closer so she can hold my hand. I roll over to face her, away from my cracks in the wall. Tara is what I need to comfort me, not the cracks in the wall.

Chapter Ten

JOSH

Josh and Alicia landed in Germany, and two soldiers greeted them at the baggage claim. The soldiers stated they would take them to the hospital in Landstuhl. Josh hadn't slept at all on the flight, even though Rodriguez had given him several sedatives to take on the flight. He couldn't bring himself to relax, let alone sleep. Alicia had been extremely quiet the entire trip but hadn't slept either. He knew she was struggling to deal with this since she had been just a baby when her mom had left for deployment. Alicia was a young woman now, having taken an accelerated high school course and had graduated early like her older sister. Now, after receiving her Bachelor's degree in social work, she had spent the last year traveling with several missionary groups to countries in need of assistance with rebuilding after hurricanes wreaked havoc on communities. He was so proud of both his girls for being able to rise above what they had been through and become successful and productive people in society.

They traded common courtesies with the soldiers and grabbed Alicia's additional suitcase she had checked in on the plane. Josh and Alicia followed the soldiers out to the street, where they had a multi-passenger van waiting for them. Josh's stomach flipped and churned, and he thought for sure he might throw up right here in the van. Once they were all in, Josh leaned his head back and closed his eyes. He felt Alicia take his hand and squeeze it. She laid her head on his shoulder, and they remained like that until they arrived at the Army base.

They pulled up in front of the hospital, and Josh saw Tara immediately sitting on a retaining wall near the curb. Tara was told what time they would arrive, but not what vehicle they would be driving. She was looking past their van, and he realized she looked at least five years older than the last time he had seen her before she left for her volunteer mission trip to Iraq. Both his daughters looked like Emily, but Tara could pass as Emily's twin. There had been times over the years as Tara had gotten older that it was difficult for Josh to look at her without seeing Emily. Alicia got out first, and Josh followed suit. As soon as they were both out of the van, it was like a sibling radar went off in Tara, and she headed their way. Alicia ran to Tara before Tara had a chance to make it to the van.

"Tara! You did it! You found mom!" Alicia pulled Tara in for one of Alicia's well-known bear hugs and rocked her side to side. Tara rubbed her sister's back and said something in Alicia's ear that Josh couldn't hear. He knew that Tara had helped Alicia create memories of their mother, even if Alicia didn't have any memories of her own. Alicia had always been Tara's biggest cheerleader and supporter of Tara's plans to find their mom one day. Even though Alicia didn't have the same passion as Tara had about finding Emily, she still believed in Tara. Josh stayed where he was on the curb as the van they had been in pulled away. After a few more minutes, Alicia finally released Tara from her bear hug grip, and they both walked over to Josh. He had tried to think about what he would say to Tara when they would meet again, but now he was utterly tongue-tied.

"Daddy..." was all that came out of Tara before she walked right into his arms for a hug and began to cry. He blinked back his tears and held her as she continued to cry. He knew without Tara even having to say anything that she had kept it together all this time. He was her safe zone, and now he would need to be strong for the three of them. "Hey there, Tara Bug, come on now. You're going to make me cry, and we both know I'm an ugly crier." She laughed through her tears and leaned back in his arms. "I love you so much, Dad. I'm sorry I couldn't tell you what was going on. But the Special Forces guys told me I had to take radio silence." Josh wiped one lonely tear away from her cheek with his thumb. "I know, Tara; you did as directed. I'm proud of your courage and patience all these years. You never gave up on your mom. Even when I thought you were chasing ghosts, you knew she was out there somewhere."

After a few more minutes outside, Tara informed both Josh and Alicia that Emily's lead doctor, Dr. Ramone wanted to meet with all three of them before they would see Emily. When Josh asked her how Emily was, Tara acted as though she didn't hear him and asked them about the flight. They followed Tara into the hospital and through the maze of hallways. Josh felt a mixture of emotions as they came to a stop in front of a closed door. Tara turned around and faced both Josh and Alicia. "Look, I know the Special Forces guys have been in touch with you, and I am sure they told you some of the details of what happened with Mom, but Dr. Ramone has some photos they took of her once she was cleaned up here in the hospital. It's important to see them before we go to see her." Tara paused and touched Josh's arm. "Especially for you, Daddy. She doesn't look much like her old self. Her eyes are still the same, but many of the features you always talked about are disfigured or scarred. It's hard to see but will help prepare you both for when you meet her in person."

Josh followed Tara and Alicia into the office of Dr. Ramone. He went through the motions of the introductions. He knew he was saying the right things by the way the doctor was nodding his head at Josh and the girls. But all Josh could focus on were the photos on the desk. Without even thinking, he reached forward and picked a picture off the desk. That's when he finally heard the doctor speaking. "Look, Josh, Emily has been to hell and beyond. Over the past decade, the injuries she has sustained have healed, but she has never had any medical treatment. She will need several surgeries once she is back in the states, but for now, we have just been focusing on helping her regain strength and get healthy. The malnutrition has caused a lot of issues for her, not to mention the continuous childbirths she has endured." Before the doctor can finish, Josh cuts him off. "You mean all the rapes, right? All the horrible sexual trauma she's been through?" Josh says this as he continues to look at the photos of Emily. Tara was right; it was hard to tell from the images in his hands that this was the love of his life. The face staring back at him was a scarred shell. The eyes were the only physical marking that could help him identify her. God, she had been in hell for all these years.

Meanwhile, he had moved on his with life. He placed the photos back on the desk and looked up at the doctor. "Are we done here? I would like to see Emily now." Dr. Ramone leads the way from his office through another maze of hallways. They stop in front of the last room on the floor. Josh couldn't help but think that the military is keeping Emily's arrival as private as possible. He knew that the media would have a field day with this story once the news was public. And the last thing Emily needed right now was to be talking to the press. The doctor looked back at Tara and then to Alicia and Josh last.

"Look, doc, we have waited fifteen years for this moment. Get out of our way now, please." Josh tacked on the 'please' at the end, hoping it would get the good doctor to move out of his way. Instead, the doctor knocked once, and then Josh heard her voice. "Come in. I'm ready." Josh could feel whatever food was left in his stomach from yesterday begin to roll around and almost thought he would throw up from nerves. He took a deep breath as the doctor opened the door for Josh and his daughters to walk in. Since Tara had already had time with Emily, she walked in and stepped to the side. Alicia, having never indeed met her mother, stayed to the side as well. Josh stepped into the room and stopped a few feet from the bed. The woman sitting up in the bed was Emily. But at the same time, it wasn't her. He couldn't stop staring at her, and he took another step closer. He didn't want to cry in front of his girls, but he knew as soon as he began to speak, the tears were going to come no matter what.

"I, I, I can't believe you're here." Josh stammered to try to keep the tears from coming. Emily wiped at her own eyes, "I really can't believe it either." She started to get out of bed, which was all it took for Josh to rush to her side. Emily scooted over in the bed, and Josh gently sat on the edge of the bed. He reached out with his right hand, nervous that if he touched her, he would hurt her. Not to mention, he was keenly aware that he wanted to respect her physical space. Emily, as if on cue, reached out with her hand and grabbed onto his hand. The instant their hands met, they both began to weep. "I want to hold you, but only if you want me to," Josh said to Emily. She nodded yes through the tears, and Josh let go of her hand and leaned forward. She fell into his arms, and it was like no time had passed at all. Emily was the love of his life, his purpose, the mother to his children. Holding her now felt right. He rubbed her back as she pressed her head into his chest. It didn't matter if she didn't look the same; she was still his Emily.

After a few minutes, Emily's tears seemed to slow down, and he could feel her breathing becoming steadier. She pulled back first and looked up at him. "I never thought I would see you again." She reached and ran a finger across his jawline. Josh wanted to lean in and kiss her, but he remembered that their daughters were in the room. Just at that moment, he heard Tara clear her throat. Both Josh and Emily looked over, and Emily leaned back with excitement. "Oh, my goodness! I am a terrible mother, Alicia, come here!" Josh stood up to get out of the way so Emily could have her turn meeting the sweet baby she had left all those years before.

Josh could tell Alicia was hesitant at first, but she walked over and took up the spot where Josh had been sitting. As soon as she sat down, Emily pulled her into an embrace. More tears, but this time from everyone. Josh stood next to Tara and leaned into her. Wanting to give Alicia and Emily some privacy, he whispered to Tara. "Let's give them a few minutes by themselves, okay?" Tara nodded, and they walked out into the hallway silently, and Josh took a deep breath. "She's alive. You found your mom." He shook his head and just stared at his brave daughter. "I'm not going to lie, Dad. I was beginning to give up on her. Nick and I had a huge argument about it, and I was beginning to think that you and him were right. But then Rosita treated her. It was like a dreamscape. Every single moment after I notified Doc and the Special Forces unit, everything I have done has felt like a dream. Even now, I feel like I am going to wake up, and I will still be in my cot, and none of this will be true." Tara's voice began to crack, and Josh brought her in for a hug. She had carried such a burden with this. She was not able to share what was going on until after the rescue. Josh wanted to take all the pain away from her. All the stress and burdens she carried, he wanted to wipe it all away for her.

Alicia came out a while later, red-eyed and blotchy-faced. Tara offered to take Alicia to the restrooms and then to grab coffee for all of them. Josh stayed behind and went back in to sit with Emily.

He had been hesitant as to when he should share with Emily how he had remarried. They had always been straightforward with each other, and Emily deserved to know. As he walked in, Emily beat him to the punch. "So, I know I'm legally dead. Tara told me I have a nice headstone." They both gave a little laugh, and it made him happy to hear Emily's old sarcasm and dark humor were still there. "You know Josh; it's okay if you moved on with your life. I can tell that isn't the wedding band we picked out together all those years ago." Ah, the wedding band. He should have known she would notice something like that. The bands they had picked out had the trinity symbol engraved around the entire wedding band. The one he wore for his marriage to Dina was a solid black metal band. As plain and simple as he could find. He stood there, fiddling with the ring on his finger.

Not sure how to say it, but in the end, he ripped the band-aid off. "I did remarry, and her name is Dina. She is an amazing woman. I'm sorry, Emily. I never gave up hope, but when the military declared you dead. I was so lost. I had the girls, and it was so much to bear." He stopped, knowing that everything he said sounded stupid compared to what she had endured in captivity. "Josh, come here." She patted the edge of the bed again, and he followed her command. Once he was seated, she grabbed his hands and looked directly into his eyes. God, her eyes were such a deep green. He could get lost in her eyes. But she brought him back to reality with her voice.

"Look, I am not upset with you. I am so messed up in my head right now; I can't even begin to process what this will mean for our family. I mean, I have eight children besides our girls. I can't imagine what that means for us either. Just know that we will figure this all out, okay?" She squeezed his hands, and he couldn't take it any longer. He leaned in and let go of her hands. He reached up and clasped a hand on each side of her face. "God, Emily, I love you so much. I have never stopped loving you." And with that, Emily leaned in, and their lips met for a tender kiss. The moment his lips met her lips, he knew his time with Dina was over. Emily was his true love, and now that he had her back, he never wanted to let her go.

Chapter Eleven

EMILY

◆━━━○━━━◆

Josh kissing me is what makes this all finally feel real. I remember early on when I would be in the hole; I would try to remember what it was like to kiss him. After so many years, I had forgotten or perhaps blocked myself from thinking about it. I just couldn't bear to think about him when I had lost all hope of ever being rescued. But now, here we are. It did break my heart to hear him say he moved on. But I can't let him see that. I can see the pain and guilt he has carried with him all these years. It's not his fault the Army gave up looking for me. He deserved to fall in love and be happy. But kissing him now, I wanted to be able to go back to the lives we had dreamed about all those years ago. I wanted to spend all my days with him and our girls. I didn't want to worry about Dina and what that would mean for us as a family. But for now, I will stay in this moment and cherish this sweet kiss.

The girls come back with coffees and some pastries for everyone. We sit around and sip on our coffee, which the girls complain about, but I think it tastes fantastic. I listen to their banter and lay back and close my eyes. I missed so much of their lives, and there is so much to learn about them. I feel an overwhelming sadness take over me. I try to snap out of it, but it's like a dark cloud lingering just over me.

"Mom, are you okay? Do you need us to get the doctor?" Tara has become my little mother hen ever since she arrived. Tara is constantly checking my vitals and reading my charts. I open my eyes and set my coffee down on the nightstand. "No, I'm okay. I just needed a minute to process this all. I love hearing you all talking, and there is just so much for me to hear about and learn. I want to get caught up right now, but I know it's going to take time. But I'm okay, I promise."

Josh and the girls stay until visiting hours are over. Then it's back to just my thoughts and the crack in the wall. I feel stronger now than when I first arrived here. Sitting up and talking to them doesn't tire me out like it did the first several days. I still don't feel like this is completely real. It's like I am waiting to hear the monster's footsteps in the doorway, and I will wake up on my mat in the corner. I begin to think about Asad, the sweet little boy who still relied on me for all his nourishments until a few weeks ago. What would become of the children? If the military confirmed that Mahir and Maimun were on the run with the monster, then the rest of the children had no one to take care of them. I overheard the nurses say that the children were here in Germany somewhere, but I had not asked about them. I am not sure I am ready to see them or decide what will happen to them. Part of me feels responsible for them. After all, I did give birth to them. But it wasn't my choice. I was raped. I was raped over and over again to produce more monsters for him. How do I move past that and raise them? How do I focus on repairing all the damage to my two daughters that thought I was dead?

My head begins to throb, and I moan quietly under my breath. I roll over away from the crack in the wall and see a folded picture on my bedside table. I unfold it, and it's a faded picture of a younger me and my sweet Tara Bug. Josh took the photo before I had left for Iraq. I flip it over and see my handwriting on the back of it. *My sweet Tara Bug, I am off to fight the monsters, but don't worry. I will be back before you know it. Love you to the moon and back, Mom.* I sit back and bring the picture to my chest and close my eyes. My sweet Tara, I don't know if I can ever recover from the guilt of leaving you for so long. I began to cry softly at first, but it quickly turned into hard sobbing. My cries are so loud that I don't even notice the nurses coming into my room. I feel someone handle my arm, and then I feel the prick of a needle, and I know they are sedating me. I continue to weep until the drugs kick in, and I feel myself drifting off to sleep.

"Roddie!! Let's go! We are the lead Humvee; we need to get out there and do our comms checks." I yell for Rodriguez at the entry to the male tent. This dude is always running late. I swear he will be late for his funeral. "I'll meet you at the truck, Sarge!" Rodriguez replies, and I roll my eyes. One day I will get this dude to listen to me, one day. I head to our makeshift motor pool. The trucks are lined up and ready to go. I see Simmons is already at our truck getting his 50-caliber machine gun set up in the mount. "Hey Simmons, how are you doing, brother?" Simmons looks down at me with those baby blue eyes and smiles a wide shit-eating grin. "It's a great day to be alive, Sarge." Simmons, my optimist. He's just a kid, but he loves this life so much. I pound the hard-shell roof of the truck, and he hits back twice—our version of a secret handshake. I get in the A-driver's seat and set up my gear. Simmons, being the hard-charging Private that he

is, has already installed our radio and has all the additional ammunition loaded in the back of the Humvee. At least I can count on him to be early and get shit done. I get out of the truck and see Rodriguez scrambling up from tent city. I smile and think about the fact that even though he drives me nuts, I love the shit out of that guy.

"Hey, Sergeant Sanders, I'm with your truck today." Our medic, Specialist Grant walks up with his medic pack on his back. "Hey Grant, glad to have you with my crew today. Why don't you plan on sitting behind Rodriguez? Simmons has the seat behind me pretty stocked up with our cooler and ammunition." Grant nods and says, "Roger that, Sarge." And he walks around to the other side of the truck. Another excellent soldier, who has proven already countless times that he not only knows his medical shit but can keep his shit together under fire. I look up at the sky, another clear sky which means that we will be sweating our asses off once the sun is entirely overhead.

I wake up in a cold sweat. I sit up and pat the bed around me and remember I am in a hospital in Germany. God, that dream was so real. It was the first time I had dreamt of Grant and Simmons so vividly. My guys. My crew. I reach over to fill my glass of water. I take a few sips and lay back down. The drugs they gave me had knocked me out. I want to go back to that memory, to before the attack. I want to remember every single detail of all three of my guys. Where were they now? And then it hits me. Even though I am in a hospital bed, I see the monsters dragging Grant in front of me. His mangled and burned body is being desiccated, and I am completely helpless. I sit back up and get up to get the motion sensor lights to turn on. I pace back and forth in my room. My visions are so clear that I feel like it's repeatedly happening; I know this is a bad sign.

I create a half-moon-like path around my hospital bed with my pacing. I have been refusing to speak with anyone in-depth about what I have gone through, but I know it's time. I don't think it's normal to have dreams like the one I had of my guys. It felt so real, and I'm scared of that. I'm afraid of what lies ahead for me. I'm safe in this room, surrounded by four walls, my crack in the wall that reminds me of my hut. What will happen when they tell me I am physically strong enough to leave? What if I am never mentally strong enough to stop chasing the ghosts that haunt my dreams. I stop at the foot of my bed and stare at the rumpled-up blankets. I need to know. I need to ask about Roddie and Simmons. I need to see them in person and talk to them. My kids and Josh being here have helped, but I need to see my guys.

I also realize that I haven't heard anything about my parents yet. God, I am a terrible daughter for not even asking Josh how they are doing. I not only need to talk to Roddie and Simmons, but I need to talk to both my parents, but especially my dad. He was always my sounding board when I needed advice and was my ultimate cheerleader. When I decided to join the Army, he was so proud of me. He went out and bought everything on the basic training packing list. He was a Korean War Veteran and had never shared much about his time in the Army. But once I graduated from basic training and AIT, that all changed. Our bond as father and daughter grew stronger with the bond of being comrades in arms.

I remember that Tara went shopping for me and had left a bag of clothes for me to try on. I hadn't been ready yet to leap my hospital scrubs to real clothes. But after my resolution to finally seek out some mental help, I think it's time to shower on my own and get dressed. I sort through the bag and immediately realize I have no idea what is in style anymore. I settle on a pair of black loose-fitted sweat pants and an olive drab-colored tee shirt. Old habits die hard, I guess. I still love the standard colors of military gear, and it makes me chuckle to myself.

I take my time in the shower. Up to this point, I have had a nurse nearby in case I lose my footing in the shower. But I want to do this on my own. I take my time, relishing that I have access to running hot water whenever I want to use it. I could take a hundred showers a day if I wanted to, and no one could stop me. The hot water rushes out of the showerhead, and I press my hands into the cold tile of the shower wall. I feel an urge to cry, and I try to bury the emotions deep down. But the tears come anyhow. I stand there, letting the hot water wash the tears away. I think about the bath I had in Iraq right before the Special Forces found me. My sweet Malika had helped me in the bath, and I remember how I relished in it, even though it was awkward having her there to witness my injuries. I know there is nothing I can do for the children, but I worry about them nonetheless. The tears finally slow down, and I finish washing my hair and body. I have so much to work on, and I am terrified of facing the demons of the hell I endured, but I know I have to face them if I want to get out of here. But I know I also need to keep it together in front of the girls and Josh. They have been through enough already without seeing me fall apart. I come back to my room and see Nurse Pierce changing out my sheets and making the bed. "Hey Pierce, I can get that. No need to be my maid too, you know." I reach for the blanket in her hands, and she pulls it back. "Now Emily, what would people say if I started letting you do my jobs for me? Plus, I'm supposed to be mad at you right now. You damn near gave me a heart attack when I came in here to check on you, and you weren't in your bed." I drop my scrubs in the laundry basket in the corner of the room and turn back around to face Pierce. "I needed to shower on my own today. I was super careful and took my time. It felt terrific to be able to do that on my own." Pierce finished making the bed and straightened up, and smiled at me. "And that is why I can't be mad at you. You are gaining strength, and that means you are one day closer to getting out of here, Emily."

I walk over to the chair next to my bed and sit down. "Pierce, can I be honest with you?" Pierce nods and sits on the edge of the bed, facing me. I take a deep breath and let it all out. I tell her how scared I am to leave these four walls. I tell her that I am beginning to dream about the guys and need to see and speak with Rodriguez and Simmons. I tell her that I'm ready to start working with the counselor, and perhaps I can begin to relay what I remember from the attack with the brass that has been patiently waiting for me to debrief. I've come to trust Pierce. She's the only nurse that doesn't shed any pity on me, and for that, I am grateful. After I unload everything on her, Pierce stands up and pulls me out of the chair. She places her hands on my shoulders, and I flinch at the touch at first, but I stay steady on my feet. She looks me square in the eyes and says, "Emily, you are beyond the strongest person I have ever met. It's not going to be easy to get through this, but if anyone can do it, it's Emily Sanders." I feel tears begin to well up in my eyes, and we both nod our heads yes, and she lets go of her hold on my shoulders and turns to walk away. She stops at the door and turns back to me. "Emily, once I walk through this door, I am going to put out the calls to Dr. Ramone, leadership, and the counselor. You are one hundred percent sure you are ready to take this step in your treatment?" I nod my head yes again, "Yes, Pierce. I am ready to carry on. Like what's written on my arm, always forward. It's the only way to go, right?" Pierce smiles and leaves. I take a deep breath and realize that today is the first day of my new life. I know I will need to work through the past, but I have to look to the future to carry on with any semblance of everyday life.

Chapter Twelve

TARA

———○———

Tara and Alicia make their way back to the hospital from the family lodge building on the hospital campus. Their dad had left before them, forever being the extreme morning person. He said he was on a mission to find their mom some healthier alternatives to the hospital food. For some reason, Tara had found that absurd because shouldn't the food they were giving their mom be healthy? But their dad was a health nut, and she was sure he had already had his diet plan to get their mom back to a stronger and healthier state.

When Tara and Alicia got up to their mom's room, Nurse Pierce stopped them in the hallway. "Hi there, ladies. You can't go in to see your mom just yet. She asked to see the therapist, and she is in there now with your mom." Tara and Alicia look at each other and back at the nurse. "Wow, that is great news. I mean, I know she has been pretty closed up about everything, so this is a step in the right direction?" Tara asks Nurse Pierce, and the kind nurse smiles and reaches out to touch Tara's arm. "Yes, Tara. This is great news and means your mom is ready to begin making progress. I'm sure Dr. Ramone will want to speak with you two and your dad later today. In the meantime, maybe you two can find her a journal, some good pens and maybe even some flowers. We don't want to put too much pressure on her to talk, and I can tell you from dealing with so many other soldiers that journaling can help them in so many ways." With that, Pierce leaves Tara and Alicia there in the hallway.

"Well," Alicia says as she gets her phone out of her bag. "I guess we get a free pass to go do some shopping." Tara smiles, knowing that this has been highly awkward for Alicia, and Alicia loves to shop, so this is the perfect escape for her. "Yes, sister. Let's go do some shopping." Tara links arms with her sister, and they turn around the way they came.

While Tara and Alicia are out shopping, Tara tries her best to stay in the moment with her sister as they look at more clothing for their mom. Alicia is going on about wanting their mom to look suitable for the return trip to the states. Tara nods and smiles, but Alicia sees through Tara's façade. Alicia throws a tee-shirt from the display table that they are both standing nearby. "Hey, jerk!" Tara yells at Alicia as she refolds it and puts it back on display. "Tara, you have been in La-La land for the past thirty minutes. Tell me what is going on in your head before I throw another shirt at you."

Alicia begins to grab another shirt from the pile, and Tara reaches for her hand. "Okay, just stop making a mess of the display." Tara starts to walk away, and Alicia follows her. Tara shakes her head and looks back at Alicia. "I wish I could be as excited as you are for mom coming home. I know this is all I have dreamed about since she went missing, but I am terrified of what will come. What if she doesn't readjust well? What will she do for work? And most of all, what is going to happen between her, dad, and

Dina?" Alicia stops walking and grabs Tara's hand. "Look, Tara, I am terrified too. And yes, I have thought about all those things as well. But guess what? Our mom is alive, and we are taking her home. Can you just revel in that for now? Can we worry about all the other things once we get back to the states? Right now, mom needs us to be strong and to remain positive. You can't let her see you worried or stressed out. She's already dealing with the burdens of coming home without us adding to it." Alicia squeezed Tara's hand and let go to check out another fashion display. Tara smiled, wondering when her baby sister turned into such a wise woman. As Alicia put it, they finished their shopping trip with more suitable outfits than the ones Tara had bought a few days ago.

When Tara and Alicia returned to the hospital, they met their dad and Dr. Ramone in the hallway outside of their mom's room. Both men had a grim look on their faces as the girls approached them. Before Tara or Alicia could say anything, Dr. Ramone spoke up. "Hey there, Tara and Alicia, why don't the four of us go back down to my office to discuss a few items that came up today." Before either Tara or Alicia could respond, the doctor and their dad walked past them and assumed the girls would follow.

The doctor takes his seat behind his desk, their dad leaning against the wall near the door, and both girls take the two available seats. Dr. Ramone continues with the doom and gloom look as he gathers some files from the top of his desk. Josh clears his throat, and Tara looks back between her dad and the doctor. "Okay, are one of you going to explain to Alicia and me what is going on?" Tara had taken Alicia's advice and had actually begun to feel a little less stressed on the way back from shopping, but now she could feel her anxiety surrounding her mom, returning to an all-time high.

Dr. Ramone stops shuffling the files back and forth on his desk. It was apparent that whatever news he had, their dad already knew, and it must be either bad news or something neither one of the men knew how to handle. Dr. Ramone finally stops fidgeting and looks up at Tara. "Tara, Alicia, your mom has begun to open up a little bit about what she has endured. I know you both are aware that she was raped multiple times and forced to bear children. She plans on giving up her maternal rights to the children and does not want to see them while they are here in Germany."

Tara sits there, staring at the doctor. She wasn't sure what he had been about to say, but this news was far from it. With all the chaos of her mom's rescue and care, Tara had forgotten entirely about the children. She closed her eyes and could picture Mahir and Maimun, the oldest two boys. They had been so helpful at the medical village. Tara realized they were still out there with that monster. She had never seen the rest of the children since Rosita had treated them. But she still felt a pang of guilt for their unknown future. Tara opened her eyes and looked over at Alicia. Alicia was looking down at her hands in her lap, clearly at a loss for words like Tara currently was.

When Tara or Alicia didn't say anything, Dr. Ramone continued. "Look, your father and I understand this is extremely difficult to process. Your mother legally has eight additional children that are all minors. With their father on the run with the oldest two boys, this leaves your mother as their sole caregiver. She has identified that she is not fit to care for these children, nor can she provide them with a stable future. They deserve a chance to a good life, and the fact that Emily can assess that shows that she is coherent and ready to begin the hard work on herself."

Tara nods her head and looks one more time from Alicia back to where her dad is standing. "Okay, you're right, Dr. Ramone. I can't even begin to process the decision my mom is making, and talking about these children reminds me of how much trauma she has survived. But I respect her decision to give up her rights to the children." Tara chokes back the tears that are forming because every time she thinks about what her mother has been through, she becomes more and more guilty for not finding her sooner. The rest of the visit with Dr. Ramone is to go over Emily's physical health. The hospital has been able to get her to a sustainable weight to travel, and her blood pressure is finally not in the dangerous low territory that it had been in when she first arrived. Dr. Ramone felt that they had done everything in Germany to get her ready to travel back to the states. He was already communicating with her new medical team at Walter Reed Hospital, where she would spend the next several months. Once she settled in the states, she would begin undergoing several reconstructive surgeries, including a double hip replacement and nerve and tissue repair to the severely scarred areas. She also had requested a total hysterectomy to be completed.

Tara remained calm while Dr. Ramone finished up explaining the next steps regarding their return flight home. Both himself and Nurse Pierce would be on the flight to monitor Emily and ensure she would remain stable. The last part about Pierce did put Tara at ease. Her mom and Pierce had developed a strong bond while her mom had been here in Germany. And the nurse was intelligent and quick on her feet. Tara had been so nervous about the long flight home, but this news made her feel more confident when they traveled home.

Tara, Alicia, and her dad left the doctor's office and began walking back down to her mom's room. Tara's dad was the one that broke the silence first. "I want you both to know that I told your mom about Dina. I don't know what the future is going to look like, but the main priority right now is getting your mom back to a healthy state both physically, mentally, and emotionally." All three of them stopped, and Tara couldn't help but ask. "Dad, have you talked to Dina at all since you got here? How is she handling all of this?" Josh crossed his arms and closed his eyes. He took a deep breath before responding. "I've talked to her once since we arrived. She's not dealing with it well at all. I think she already has it in her head that we will get a divorce."

Tara couldn't even begin to think about the choices her dad would have to make in the next few months. He was legally married to Dina, but he was also married to Emily, even though her mom had been declared deceased. What a mess this all was. But her dad was right; the most important item right now was for them all to focus on her mom's recovery. Tara made a mental note to email Doc back in Iraq tonight. She would need to let him know that she would not be returning and would need someone to pack up the rest of her items to have shipped home.

Chapter Thirteen

JOSH

After sharing with the girls where Josh was with his relationship with Dina and Emily, he was beyond emotionally spent. He was trying so hard to remain strong and calm throughout everything, but it took a toll on him. His main priority was getting Emily home and beginning her full recovery. When he arrived at the hospital today, and Dr. Ramone had intercepted him to let him know that Emily was starting to open up about her experiences, he had been relieved for that. It wasn't that she was being stubborn about talking, but more like she was in a state of numbness about everything. Even though he could never even try to relate to what she had been through as a prisoner for so long, he did understand the numbness and closing herself off to everyone. He was ready to wait for her to talk to him about it and would continue to wait for however long it would take. He just wasn't sure what that would mean for his marriage to Dina.

Josh knocked on Emily's door before opening it. Hearing her voice come through the other side still gave him the same feelings he had all those years ago when he first met her. Josh opened the door, and she was sitting up in bed, her left leg tucked in but her right leg straight out. He knew her right side was the root of a lot of her physical issues. She more than likely had dislocated her hip when the Humvee had rolled over, and she had suffered from severe third-degree burns to both calves and feet, but her right one had pretty bad scarring. Emily looked exhausted, and he was about ready to say he would come back later when that classic Emily smile appeared.

"Hey, guys! I thought you three were never going to show up today. Kind of figured you changed your minds about hanging out with me." Emily winked at Josh, and he was immediately speechless. Even while recovering from being a prisoner of war, her charisma could still light up a room. Alicia plopped down on the edge of the bed and leaned in to kiss her mom. "Mom! Please, are you kidding us? There is nowhere else in the world we would rather be. Plus, I had to take Tara shopping for you. From what you have been sporting from her last shopping trip proved just how badly you needed a real fashion consultant to come to the rescue."

Josh took up his standard post of leaning up against the wall while Tara went over to the chair and handed the shopping bags over to Alicia. As surreal as it was to have all three of his women in one room, Josh had to admit it felt good. It felt right. And he couldn't believe how quickly Alicia and Emily had bonded. It was as if Emily had never even been gone from Alicia's entire life. Even though Tara was the carbon copy of Emily, Alicia had Emily's charisma and magical way to make everyone fall in love with her. He stayed there in the corner just watching Alicia show Emily all the items they had purchased that morning for Emily. He loved how Alicia had a story about each piece, and every so often, Emily would look up at him and give him that radiating smile again.

Josh felt his phone going off in his pocket and snuck out without any of his ladies even noticing. It was Rodriguez calling. "Hey, Roddie. Sorry man, I lost track of time and have been meaning to call you." Josh figured he would just get the apology out of the way since he had promised to keep Rodriguez up to date on what was going on. But the truth was that every night since he had been here, by the time he would get back to his room, he would just crash. Some nights, he would pass out fully dressed.

"Bro, don't even sweat it. I can only imagine how overwhelming and crazy it has been for all of you. No, I'm calling because the hospital called me. They wanted to see if I could meet you all at Walter Reed. I guess Emily was asking about Simmons and me. Of course, no one in Germany wanted to tell her that Simmons was dead. I guess the Brass over there thought it makes way better sense for me to break that news to her." Rodriguez, always the smartass, of course, had to throw in a jab at leadership. "Are you going to be good with that, Roddie? I mean, I know how hard it's been for you since he died. I can tell her if you want me to." As much as Josh did not want to be the one to tell Emily that Simmons had taken his own life after years of battling drug addiction to pain pills due to the guilt of never finding Emily, he would if that would help his best friend. "No, man, I need to do this. You and Emily have a special bond as husband and wife, but me and Emily, our bond is different. I was there when shit went down, and I was the last one to talk to Simmons before his shit went down. I can handle it."

Josh shared with Rodriguez the details for their return flight home. Since Roddie was out of the military, he would need to arrange his flight to D.C.

They finished up the call, and Josh headed back into Emily's room. Emily must have been trying on her new outfits and hosting a fashion show when he walked in. She was currently standing near the bathroom door, holding on to the trim while Alicia finished buttoning up the blouse Emily had on. Still sitting in the chair, Tara looked at Alicia with her older sister's 'judge' face as they used to call it when the girls were younger. "I told you buttons were a bad idea. Easy tee shirts and sweats, that's what mom needs right now. Right, Mom?" Tara looked to Emily, and Emily looked to Josh. Even with her hair turning a silvery gray, she was still so beautiful. "You know, your mom could be wearing rags, and she would still be the most beautiful woman in the room." Josh couldn't help himself; he walked over to Emily and gave her a small peck on the cheek, and brushed the hair away from her face.

Alicia stepped aside and cleared her throat. "Okay, you two.... Get a room or something. We may be your adult daughters, but that doesn't mean we need to see you making out." Alicia nudged Josh in the side and went over to take up her spot back on the bed. "Well, since your dad brought up wearing rags, I am used to wearing them. But I LOVE all my new clothes. Thank you, Alicia and Tara, for taking the time to shop for me. Once the doctors clear me from the hospital, you will have so much to teach me about what's in style. And even how to use those fancy phones you all have. Gosh, when I left, I think we were still using flip phones." Emily leaned into Josh's hand as he continued to rub his thumb against her cheek. He could tell she was getting more comfortable with touch, and that made his heart swell even more.

Josh hesitated if he should tell Emily who had called him when she beat him to the punch. "So, who was that on the phone just now?" Josh smiled, excited and nervous to tell her. "Well, Miss Nosey," He grabbed both her hands and kissed her knuckles. "That was the one and only Rodriguez. He wanted me to tell you that he will be meeting us at Walter Reed when you arrive." The look on Emily's face was priceless. She brought her hands, still linked to Josh's, to her face, and tears filled her eyes. "Oh, wow! That is amazing! I've had dreams about the guys, and I told the doctors I need to see and talk to Roddie and Simmons. I think that will help me with moving past a lot of this." Emily looked away, and Josh could tell she was trying so hard to stay strong for him and the girls.

"Hey girls, can you two give us a minute?" Josh didn't even look over at Tara and Alicia, but he could hear them get up and walk out of the room. "Is it okay if I wrap my arms around you?" The counselor had been working with Josh on how to help Emily, and one of the biggest things they told him was to ask her permission before touching her. Her sexual traumas were not something she would get over quickly. Emily, still turned away from Josh, nodded her head. Josh gently brought his arms around her, and she fell into his chest without any apprehension. He rubbed her back and said, "Look, I know you are trying to keep it together for us, but you can let your wall down with me. I promise you are safe with me." It was as if Emily needed that permission to let go. He could feel her body begin to shake as the cries started, softly at first and then louder. They stood there, Josh holding Emily while she let out years of emotions she had been suppressing.

Josh had lost track of time, standing there, holding Emily while she got out everything she had been holding in. Her shoulders finally stopped moving, and she pulled her face away from his chest. "I'm sorry. I guess I needed that. Thank you for being here for me." Emily looked exhausted, so Josh took her over to the bed so she could lie down. "Don't ever apologize for anything, do you hear me? You can always be open with me; you know that, right?" Josh helped her to bed and covered her up with the sheet. She rolled over towards the wall, and he followed her stare to the crack in the wall. She lifted her hand and began tracing the crack. "Josh, I'm scared to leave this room. I don't know how I am going to react when the world opens back up to me."

Josh hearing what Emily had just said crushed his heart. He sighed and gently sat on the edge of the bed. "Emily, I know you may not think this, but you are the strongest human being alive. I will never fully understand what you have been through, but I am pretty sure you have been to hell and back. You're right; it's going to be overwhelming once we get back to the states. But the one thing I do know is that I will be right by your side the entire time. Tara and Alicia too. We will be there to support you in whatever way you need from us. So even though there are a lot of unknowns for you, you have to know that we are a family unit, and you will get through this."

Emily reached over and grabbed Josh's hand. She squeezed it, and he squeezed back. "I never stopped loving you, Josh Sanders. Even though I had to shut you all out of my head for a long time, I never stopped loving you in my heart." Josh dropped his head down, her words making the guilt he already felt so much heavier. He should never have given up hope on her. How could Josh have let himself fall in love and marry another woman? He tucked those emotions down deep; this was Emily's time, and he could not make this about him and what he was going through. He knew he still had an entirely different life at home he would have to face. But for now, that would have to wait. He had given up on Emily once before, and he sure as hell would not let that happen again.

Chapter Fourteen

EMILY

I feel the cold dirt under my cheek, and I stretch out my left arm to probe into the darkness. The darkness is like a dark cloud shrouding my eyes, and I have no idea where they have taken me. I open my mouth to cry out, but my throat is so dry. I close it and try to swallow, but there is no saliva in my mouth to coat my throat. My right arm is tucked under me, and when I try to move, there is a searing pain that shoots out from my right shoulder and travels up and down the entire right side of my body. The pain is what gets my vocal cords working. I scream a horse cry, fueled by the pain. After a while, the pain subsides, and I try again to make my body move, but the pain completely paralyzes me. This time though, not only is there a stabbing pain moving up and down my right side, but my head begins to throb something fierce. I pull my left arm back in and rub my forehead, and that's when it all begins to come back to me. I can stick three fingers width into the gash. God, that's not good. I press my right cheek against the cold dirt floor again. It gives some relief from the pain in my head. I try to force myself to stay awake, but I can feel my eyes begging to close again. All I can hope for is that I don't wake back up.

"Mom, where did you go?" I hear Tara's voice behind me, and I shake my head. The memories of all those years in hell have been coming back to me more and more. Ever since I began talking to the counselor, it's like this flood gate has opened, and I can't stop the memories from coming back. I shake my head and turn to face her. "I'm sorry, Tara Bug, I just spaced out for a minute. The doctors think it's a lingering side effect from my head injuries. I'm here. I'm good to go." I hand her the shirt I had been folding, and she packs it into an Army duffle bag. I mean, I'm not lying to her about spacing out. It kind of is a lingering side effect from my injuries, just more or less the trauma side of it all.

For the last two days, everyone talked and made plans for my return trip while I just sat back and listened. I appreciate Tara and Josh taking the lead, but it almost feels like I am just a fly on the wall watching what is happening around me and not a part of the plans. But I am the plans. For the most part, the media is keeping its distance. The Army did their best to keep my rescue top secret, but it leaked back to the states like these missions always do. I was shocked to learn that Donald Trump is President of the United States. I asked Josh, 'Isn't he a like a scum bag millionaire or something?' Josh just laughed and shook his head and told me I had so much to catch up on. The plans were to leave Germany and fly back to Washington D.C., where a whole dog and pony show would be waiting for me on the tarmac. Nurse Pierce would be traveling with us, and I am so grateful for this. She assured me that she would have some anxiety meds on hand if it all got to be too much for me.

"Mom, you know you can talk to me about what happened to you. I'm not a little girl anymore. I can handle it." Tara closed up the duffle bag and crossed her arms over her chest. She was right. She was not the little girl I walked away from all those years ago. Standing in front of me now was a strong, intelligent, and beautiful woman, who is why I am here today. She might think she can handle my flashbacks, but that is not her burden to carry. "Look, Tara, I love you with my entire heart and soul. I know you are here for me and want to help. And you are helping me so much. I am handling it, and I'm just not ready to share every detail with you or your sister, or your dad yet. I may be able to in time, but the best way you can help me is to give me the space to process it all. Okay, Tara Bug?" Tara nodded, and I opened up my arms for her to come in for a hug. I was getting better with physical contact and not cringing every time someone touched me. The counselor said this was significant progress and that if I felt comfortable with a person, that I should be the one to make an effort for contact. Hugging Tara is effortless, though. I rub her back, and she lays her head on my shoulder. She might be a strong young woman, but she will always be my sweet baby girl.

I let Tara go, and we finished packing up what few belongings I had. It occurs to me that the medical team must have thrown the rags I wore when I arrived away. The thought of this makes me sad for a moment, but then I remember those pieces of fabric only stand to remind me of my years in hell. The only item left on my list of to-dos was to sign off of my parental rights to those sweet children. I know they are here within military control, and the Army was working with social workers and immigration to determine the best next steps. Part of my heart broke for the children, but the doctors and counselors all agree that I am making the right choice. The children deserve a chance at a new beginning, and I do not have the means or emotional connection to care for them.

"Okay, I think that is it, Mom. Are you ready to head down to Dr. Ramone's office? I think Dad and Alicia are already down there." Tara slings the duffle bag over her shoulders, and I grab the small backpack she bought for me. I look around one last time, the only actual room I have known since before being captured. I take one last look at the crack in the wall, which has brought me so much comfort since arriving. "Yes, I am ready to go. I'm ready to go home."

As we begin walking down the hall, I realize this is my first time outside my room. I have a cane to help me walk since my right leg is shorter than my left. That will be my first surgery once we are back in the states. A total hip replacement on both sides will hopefully allow me to get back to walking with no pain and eventually without the cane. Next up, they will work on the scar tissue in my right leg and potentially correct some nerve damage from all the burns and shrapnel. I told the doctors that I vaguely remember an older woman caring for my wounds early on, and she would pick out pieces of shrapnel. She would have me bite down on a strap of leather because there were no pain meds. That was only one of the times I made Dr. Ramone speechless. I am confident I am his first rescued prisoner and hopefully will be his last.

We turn the corner of the hallway, and medical staff is lining both sides of the hallway. They are all smiling as we approach, and it dawns on me that they are here for me. Tara touches my left elbow, and I look at her and smile. "You still okay, Mom?" She asks, worried that this will be too much for me. "I guess so. Plus, this is practice for what I can expect once we land, right?" I smile and wink at her, reminding myself that I have to remain strong not only for her but for everyone. I don't want the public to think those bastards made me weak. I smile at everyone as we pass, muttering the occasional 'Thank you' and nodding my head at others.

Tara stops in front of a door with the nameplate for Dr. Ramone on it. She opens the door, and inside it's a packed room. Josh is standing over in the corner with Alicia while the doctor is standing behind his desk. Sitting in one of the chairs is my counselor, who is also the liaison for the children. She motions for me to take the seat next to her, and I gladly accept. I haven't been walking that much, and the trek down the hall tired me out more than I thought it would.

"Emily, have you had a chance to read over these documents? And if so, do you understand what you are signing?" The counselor pushes the stack of papers back before me, and I pick them up, but I already know what they say. "Yes, I have had nothing but time to review them. I am ready to sign them so you can begin finding the kids a good family." She nods her head and hands me a pen. I flip to the pages that she has sticky notes on, and I sign on the respective lines. In all honesty, even though I am their birth mother, I don't feel like I ever had any rights over them. The monster only wanted to breed me for the sake of building up his army, which, considering Mahir and Maimun were still on the run with him, shows that to be true. I hand the paperwork and pen back to the counselor. I nodded my head, and she patted my arm. We have talked about this a lot over the past few days. She said that this was a step towards rebuilding my new life. I repeat that to myself- my new life. It's so odd to say this phrase, but she's right. The old Emily Sanders was buried in Arlington Cemetery. The old Emily was beaten, raped, and held prisoner for close to fifteen years. I don't know who the new Emily will be, but I have to begin accepting what was done to me to move on to the future.

Dr. Ramone wrapped up the meeting by handing over my medical files to me. He made copies of everything so there would be no issues once we arrived at Walter Reed Hospital. I look over at Josh, standing in the office corner with his arms folded across his chest. Even though he kept his hair in the standard military high and tight, I could see the grey hairs coming in. The years had aged him, and I felt an overwhelming urge to get up and hug him. He carried the burden of my imprisonment on his shoulders. He looks up at me and winks, and even though I have so much sadness and anxiety going through my head, I know that I can get through this as long as he is with me.

After we discuss the rest of the logistics, it's time to leave. All of a sudden, I feel a wave of emotions come over me. I grab onto the armrests of the chair I am sitting in and grip on tight. I feel a hand gently tap my shoulder. "Mom, are you alright?" It's Tara, my mother hen always paying attention to any sudden movement I make. I don't answer her right away, so she comes around to the left side of the chair and kneels next to me. I am paralyzed with fear, and I can't even speak. Others notice, and now I hear lots of talking, and people are moving around.

Nurse Pierce and Dr. Ramone asked my family to leave for a moment. Having everyone leave was a good call as the room was beginning to close in on me. The counselor remains, and I hear her call my name several times. I finally find the strength to turn my head to look at her. "Emily, what you are experiencing right now is completely natural. I want you to think about what you're feeling and stop trying to block those emotions. I want you to feel the positive and the negative emotions together. Can you do this for me?" I nod my head and close my eyes. We have been working on this. She says that I am trying too hard to be strong for everyone, and suppressing the emotions will only lead to a breakdown later on. I acknowledge the emotions I am feeling.

I'm excited to get back to the U.S., anxious about the flight, and terrified of leaving this hospital. I also feel guilty for leaving the children behind, but I am also relieved that they are no longer my responsibility. I let all the emotions and thoughts come out. Embracing each one and then letting them go. It's not easy, and I feel my heart beating faster, but I push through. I finally open my eyes and feel myself letting go of the death grip I had on the chair. I look from my counselor to Nurse Pierce, to Dr. Ramone. "I can do this, guys. I know I can." And with that, Dr. Ramone walks around from his side of the desk and opens the door. "Alright, Sgt. Sanders, then you have a plane to catch. You are going home."

They bring me a wheelchair to leave the hospital in, but I refuse to use it. I am going to walk out of this hospital on my own two feet. No matter how hard it is and how tired I get. I mean, if I get tired, I will just sleep on the plane anyhow. As we leave the hospital, staff and even patients poke their heads out of rooms and offices to catch a peek of the imprisoned soldier. Since being here in Germany, I have refused to watch any television because I don't want to know what the media says. The military chain of command has instructed me on what I can and cannot say to the media. I have no desire to share my story or even comment with anyone outside of my family and team of medical professionals.

We walk out of the hospital, and it's the first time I have been outside since my imprisonment. I stop in my tracks and look around. I knew we were on a military base, but I hadn't seen real civilization in so long. Tara and Josh, one on each side of me, simultaneously put a hand to my lower back. Tara leans in and whispers to me, "Are you okay? Do you need to sit down?" I look at her with tears in my eyes and say, "No, honey, I feel great. I haven't seen the real world in so long. I just need a minute to capture everything."

I hear Josh clear his throat, and he begins to rub my back. Tara leans her head on my shoulder very gently. "I love you, Mom." Now it's my turn to take my arm and wrap it behind her back. "I love you too, Tara Bug." I nod my head and motion to keep moving forward. I take the steps down to the SUV slowly. I am still getting used to walking and not wanting to look weak in front of the military entourage waiting for us in front of the all-black SUVs.

"SGT Emily Sanders, it has been our privilege and honor to serve you here at Landstuhl Regional Medical Center." The officer in front of me holds out his hand for me to shake it. I slowly shift my cane to my left hand and bring my right arm up to salute him. He was not expecting me to follow military protocol, and he quickly brought his hand up to reciprocate the salute. "Thank you, sir, for everything. You run an excellent hospital, and everyone has taken such good care of me." I vaguely remember him from the day I began sharing details of my captivity. He must be the presiding officer over the hospital.

The other officers standing with him take turns shaking my hand, and then they part ways to make my way into the SUV. Tara, Alicia, and Josh all get in the back with me, and I see Dr. Ramone and Pierce get into another SUV. Tara grabs my hand, and I squeeze it. I look at each one of them, and I can tell they are nervous and excited. "I'm okay, everyone. I promise. I just want to get home."

We ride in silence to the hangar where the plane is waiting for us. The military did not want to risk us flying on a standard aircraft, so the military had a private plane plus my medical team for the four of us. I feel the anxiety beginning to rise in the pit of my stomach again. The last time I was on a plane was when I went to Iraq for my deployment all those years ago. As if he could read my mind, Josh turns around from where he is sitting and gives me that smile that has always warmed my heart. I nod at him and return the smile. Even after all these years, it's like we have picked back up where we left off. No words are shared; I know he told me everything would be alright and let the anxiety go. I have to keep reminding myself that he is married and in love with another woman. If I don't remind myself of this, I may slip too far back into being Mrs. Emily Sanders.

Chapter Fifteen

TARA

Tara looked from her mom to her dad, and for a split second, it felt as though they were all just heading on a family vacation and not bringing her mom back from captivity. She knew this had to be beyond difficult for her mom, but she handled it all like a strong woman. And Tara's dad, along with Tara and her sister, was right there to support Emily every step of the way. Watching the silent interaction between her parents made Tara happy and sad for what was in store for them when they landed stateside. Tara's dad had been honest about Dina with Emily. And while they had been in Germany, Tara knew that he had called Dina several times to give her updates. Surprisingly, Dina was incredibly supportive of the situation. In some ways, Tara wondered if she had a choice. It was a no-brainer to Tara and Alicia that their dad would be divorcing Dina as soon as possible now that their mother was alive.

As they boarded the plane, Tara helped with the baggage to give herself something to do. She wasn't afraid to fly, but she just had a terrible sense of anxiety overwhelm her. Alicia came to the back of the SUV and grabbed a bag just as Tara was reaching for it. "Hey, you know you don't have to be the rock for all of us. You can take a break from being the savior." Tara stops and turns to face Alicia head-on. "Is that what you think? That I am purposely like this? If you haven't noticed, Alicia, our mother, who has been missing for over fifteen years, is about to fly back home to the government that declared her dead. Sorry if I act as though I have to be strong. I'm not doing it for you. I'm doing it for myself. Do you see how much of a badass she is? She is keeping it together so well when all I want to do is fall apart and cry. If you came over to talk shit or start something, just walk away now." Tara grabs the last bag from the SUV and walks away from her little sister before she tries to get in the last word.

Tara loved Alicia, but sometimes that girl could push Tara's buttons as no one else could. Nick told her all the time about how Tara needed just to learn to let it go. But Alicia would keep pushing and pushing until Tara would snap or say something like she just had to her. They always made up; that was the best part of being sisters, being able to hate each other one minute and love each other the next. Tara was the last one to enter the plane. It was a smaller private jet, and the Army had not held back on luxury. The main cabin was like a living room, with recliner like seating and enough leg space that even her tall fiancé would appreciate. God, she wished Nick could have flown out to Germany to be with her. She had finally connected with Nick after several missed attempts on his end. She had to wait for him to call the hospital or her room, but she was always at the wrong place the first few times when he had tried calling her.

Nick had reassured her that everyone at the medical village was safe. Doc was working on getting replacements for Tara, Nick, and Rosie. Both Nick and Rosie wanted to be in D.C. when Tara and her family landed. Unfortunately, replacements took time to find and to relocate to Iraq. She had reassured him that she knew if he could be there, he would be, and she 100% understood the logistic issues. He promised they would be stateside as soon as possible.

Tara had asked about Mahir and Maimun, and Nick had paused longer than he should have. She could sense he knew something and didn't want to tell her. Mahir and Maimun had indeed taken up fighting against the U.S. soldiers when they had infiltrated the village to rescue her mom. They somehow had escaped, and no one had heard from them or seen them in weeks. Learning this news broke Tara's heart because she knew deep down, they were good boys. It wasn't their fault they were born and bred to become soldiers. They had been on her mind ever since that conversation with Nick. Even now, Tara couldn't help but think about all the children and what would become of them. Her mother had made the right choice by signing over her rights of the kids, but what's next? It made her sad to think the rest of them would be split up and potentially separated in different countries. Tara shook her head and had to convince herself to stop thinking about them. They were not her concern. Her main concern was getting her mom back to the states.

Tara watched her mom across from her get settled in next to Alicia. Tara still found it interesting how Alicia and her mom had fallen right into their relationship. If someone hadn't known the whole story, you would have no way of knowing Alicia had been separated from her mother when she was still a baby. Alicia had been working with their mom on how to use an iPhone. Emily was not the greatest at it, considering that flip phones and iPods were the latest trends when she had left for Iraq. It was endearing to watch Alicia teach their mom something on the phone. Emily's eyesight was not the greatest, so she held the phone at an awkward arm's distance away from her. Tara couldn't understand what they were saying with the jet engines running, but Alicia must have said something funny since they were both laughing. And that is when Tara's heart stopped. Her mother's laugh. That infectious laugh could bring a smile to the grumpiest person's face. Tara's dad heard it, too, from his seat next to Tara. They both stared at Emily in awe while straining to listen to her laugh over the engines. She wasn't sure if her mom would be like her old self. Even though her mom was still coming to terms with what she had been through, for the most part, she was the mom Tara had remembered all those years ago.

Chapter Sixteen

JOSH

—◇—

Josh couldn't stop staring at Emily as her laugh enveloped the plane. Even though she had been through so much, her laugh remained the same. He could feel a smile spread across his face as her laughter was now in surround sound, with Alicia and Tara both joining in. He had no idea what Alicia said to cause the laughter, and it didn't matter. Josh had his family back, and his heart was full to the brim with love and happiness. Josh made eye contact with Emily, and she winked at him, which made his heart melt in his chest. She was his soulmate. He had no clue how he was going to return to Dina and face her.

A male voice came over the speakers to announce that the jet would begin moving into position on the tarmac for takeoff. Since they were on a private jet on a military base, it wasn't quite like flying in coach on a civilian airplane. Their flight attendant went around the cabin to ensure each passenger buckled in and took drink orders. When the flight attendant got to Emily, she lightly touched Emily's hand, making Emily flinch. The flight attendant began to apologize repeatedly, and Dr. Ramone motioned for her to come to his seat. From where Josh was sitting, he could tell the good doctor was filling the flight attendant in on the situation and their special passenger.

Josh looked back to Emily, who was sitting next to Alicia. He could tell Alicia was probably talking Emily through what had just happened, trying to keep her anxiety in check since they were all so close to takeoff. Emily had refused to take any sort of medication to calm her nerves. She said she did not want to numb her emotions, and both her counselor and Dr. Ramone had agreed that as long as Emily could manage these episodes appropriately, they would agree on no medications. But Josh knew the good doctor had brought a variety of drugs just in case Emily needed them.

Emily looked at Josh again, and this time it was his chance to wink at her. Their silent signal to each other was their code. Being a married couple in the military, they had never been big on public displays of affection, so winking was their way to say I love you without saying anything at all. She smiled and laid her head back on the headrest. She took a deep breath and closed her eyes as she reached for Alicia's hand. Alicia looked down, surprised, but he could tell it made her happy. She squeezed gently and kept her hand in place. They were all learning that any touch or physical interactions with Emily would have to be on her terms. Patience would be vital in helping her work through all the years of imprisonment and trauma.

Josh was grateful that Dr. Ramone was flying with them to Walter Reed since he had been Emily's doctor since she had landed in Germany. Both Dr. Ramone and Nurse Pierce had gained Emily's trust, and Dr. Ramone believed that she would need strong advocates on the medical side once they landed. Walter Reed was one of the best US military hospitals, but medical files could only tell part of the patient's story. Josh couldn't agree more with the doctor and knew that Emily would receive the best care the military had to offer.

The private jet taxied onto the runway, and they prepared for takeoff. Before Josh knew it, the plane was 40,000 feet above sea level, crossing the Atlantic Ocean and heading back home. Josh and his daughters were taking Emily home. It was a surreal thought, but yet it was real and not a dream. In less than ten hours, they would be in Washington D.C., where Emily would receive the hero welcome she deserved.

Josh tried to shut his mind off during the flight, but he couldn't take his eyes off Emily. She had fallen asleep fairly quickly after they were in the air. Alicia had helped her with a neck pillow, and the flight attendant had gently placed a blanket over Emily, which Alicia helped get into place. She was resting peacefully, her lips slightly parted, and he could tell when she had reached the deep sleep state. Her breathing slowed down, and Emily took deeper breaths. The crease lines in her forehead softened, and she looked peaceful. Josh tried not to think about all the shit she had endured. But he had been in the room for some of Emily's statements to the higher-ranking officers. It was beyond sick what she had endured. He had always known she was a strong woman, capable of anything. Still, the torture, the rapes, the isolation, and starvation were beyond anything he could ever comprehend any human surviving. During her interviews with the brass, one colonel had asked her why she hadn't tried to kill her captor and run. Emily replied without any hesitation and said, "And go where sir? You and the entire Army had stopped looking for me. Where could I have gone if I had escaped him?" All the officers had looked down at their clipboards and cleared their throats, knowing they had to tread lightly with Emily. She was correct; had she killed her captor and ran away, she had no lifeline or escape route. They had kept her underground for most of the first few years of her imprisonment. By the time she lived in the hut, the Army had all but given up any search and rescue operations.

As much as Josh wanted to be with Emily at Walter Reed, part of him wished he could reenlist and join the efforts to track down Mohammad Baz and his small army. He wanted revenge more than anyone else, and he could picture himself being the one to capture that bastard for everything he had done to his wife. But Josh knew that the Army would never grant his wish. Even if he wasn't retired and was still active-duty Army, he was too close to the situation to be part of the mission. That was the same way it had been with all the search and rescue missions back when Emily and Grant had gone missing. He was kept stateside for close to two years and had to undergo counseling before clearing him ready for combat.

Josh refocused on Emily sleeping across from him. She had aged so much from everything she had been through, yet she was still the most beautiful woman he had ever seen. He closed his eyes and forced himself to think of a happier time. He thought about when they had moved into military housing shortly after their modest military wedding. Neither one of them had been approved for any time off, so they were moving the limited personal belongings they had after working all day. He laughed at the memory of him picking Emily up to cross through their front doorstep that first time. She was not having it since they were both in their uniforms. But Josh didn't care one bit. She was his bride, and even if they couldn't have a traditional wedding, he was going to do this part right. She punched his chest and tried to push him away, but no matter what she said, he was stronger than her, and he won in the end. He gently placed her down in their stark living room, and they kissed right there with the front door open and all of the military base to see. Had he known those days were going to be so limited, he would have burned into his brain every single second they had spent with each other. He spent years filled with regret for not having more memories of Emily, and now that he had her back, he couldn't imagine leaving her side for one second. He opened his eyes and knew what he would have to do when they landed. He had to leave Dina for good, which would be difficult, but it was the right thing to do.

Chapter Seventeen

EMILY

—◦—

I woke up to the jolt of the private jet landing. I looked out my window and took in a deep breath. It occurred to me that I was in the United States. I closed my eyes and tried to choke back the tears that were already straining to come out. I exhaled slowly and opened my eyes, and reached for Alicia's hand. She had been so patient with me this entire flight. Whenever I felt the panic or nausea from my anxiety hitting me, her hand was there, ready to be held and squeezed. I held on to her hand, and she held on right back. She leaned over to me and whispered, "Welcome Home, Mama." That was it; the tears I was trying so hard to keep back flowed freely. Tara and Josh look over at me, and I force out a weak smile for them. Tara unbuckles herself and rushes over to kneel in front of me. "Mom, it's okay. You're safe. You are finally home."

I nod to her, and with my other hand, I reach forward for her hand. "I know Tara Bug. That's just it, I never thought I would make it home, yet here I am. I have so many emotions running through me right now, and I guess crying is the only way I can express them all." I look over to Josh, who stays in his seat. I can tell he is taking this moment in from the look on his face. I give him our secret code through one wink, and he winks back.

We wait for the flight attendant to let us know when we can begin unloading. Since this is a private jet, we will exit on the tarmac versus going straight into the airport. The military is doing its best to keep my homecoming quiet, which was at my request. I did not want the pomp and circumstance of a traditional military ceremony. I just wanted to get to Walter Reed Hospital so I could continue with my medical care. But more than getting the medical treatment that I know I need, I want to go to my gravesite.

Ever since I found out that I was given a proper burial at Arlington National Cemetery, all I could think about was that I was a walking, talking ghost. Technically speaking, I was buried six feet underground in an empty coffin. I told Josh that I had understood why they had followed through with a funeral, but in reality, I didn't understand. I could see how Tara couldn't let this go for her entire life. How could you bury an empty coffin based on the fact that another soldier's remains had been found and not mine?

We exited the jet, and there were blacked-out SUVs just like the ones we had ridden in Germany. Several soldiers were waiting for us as we approached the SUV. We stopped in front of them, and with one fluid movement, they all saluted me. I shook my head and laughed, "Soldiers, no need to salute me. I used to work for a living." They all smiled as they lowered their salute. At least I hadn't lost my sense of humor. It was a long-standing joke in the military that non-commissioned officers like myself and Josh worked for a living, which was more than one could say about officers. It seemed as though my joke helped lighten the mood, and it was a heavy reminder that my family and my medical team are watching every move I make and listening to every word I say. If I want to get past this medical treatment, I need to be the person they want me to be. I stuffed down my anxiety and put a weak smile on my face. Let's get this dog and pony show on the road.

The rest of the day and even the week go by in a blur. Tests after tests, consult after consults. I have a team of doctors and specialists planning the next six to twelve months of surgeries and recovery. I am a medical and military miracle to so many people. How could one human withstand over a decade of torture, rapes, and pregnancies? I keep my strong face on and wait every evening until visiting hours are over before I gather my blanket and head to the corner of the hospital room. Backing into the corner of the room, I slowly slide down to the floor where I huddle as I used to in the hut. Sitting like this is what soothes me and keeps me going. I need this reminder of my past if I want to face the future.

Most mornings, Nurse Pierce finds me huddle on the floor and gently wakes me up, and I stumble back to my bed. If she has reported my actions to Dr. Ramone, I have not heard about it yet. I have a feeling she has not said anything about my sleeping arrangements. Pierce has become a true friend since I first met her strapped down to the bed in Germany.

"Today is a big day for you, Emily," Pierce says as she gets out my hygiene kit and towels from the cabinet near my bathroom. I roll over to face her, and even though I know what she is talking about, I somehow can't find any words to respond. Pierce looks over her shoulder at me, and she can sense something is not right with me. She comes over to the bed and nods at it to sit down. I move my legs over so she has room to sit on the edge of the bed.

"Emily, if you don't want Rodriguez to come today, I'm sure we can reschedule the meeting." I push myself up to a sitting position and look down at my hands. "No, I want to see him. Plus, I have already postponed meeting him twice. Josh told me he'd been here since the day I arrived. I can't keep him waiting any longer." Pierce sighed, and I know she is choosing her words carefully. "Look, Emily, you don't have to do anything you do not want to do. Everyone here is in your corner and supports you, and trust me, Rodriguez is at the top of the list.

I look up at her and nod my head in agreement. I know I have the best medical team and family supporting me. But I do feel a weight so heavy to recover faster than I think I can handle. "I want to see him today. And then Josh and I are going to Arlington later this afternoon. I need to see it. I need to see where I am buried and pay my respects to Grant." Now it was Pierce's turn to look down at her hands, and she nodded her head. "Sgt. Emily Sanders, you are the strongest person I have ever met. Have I told you that lately?" We both let out a laugh, "Okay, enough of all this, let me get in the shower and get this day going."

After I finish getting ready, I get my room cleaned up. I refuse to be completely useless. I insist on making my bed, taking care of my trash, and sweeping the room. My medical team agrees that this is good for me and the hospital cleaning staff begrudgingly allows me to do some of their jobs. Once I get all my morning chores done, I sit down at the chair near the window and grab my journal. I have been documenting everything since arriving here in the states. All my interactions, emotions, and flashbacks, whether they are when I am awake or asleep. Roddie will not come for another hour, and I need some time to clear my head.

Tuesday, August 20, 2019

I slept in the corner again. I know I need to sleep in the bed, but I feel safer in the corner. As much as I don't miss being a prisoner in that hut, I miss my bedding. I miss my crack in the wall, and I miss tending to the children. I have been feeling the guilt of giving them up more and more. I know it was the right thing to do, but I feel like they have no chance for a better life now. Maybe I should have requested them to be granted their visas and be allowed to come to D.C. with me. I know at some point Pierce is going to have to tell someone about my sleeping routine. If she tells, this will set me back in my treatment. The shrinks think I am doing so well, but in reality, I am a mess.

I guess it doesn't matter much. I will be undergoing my double hysterectomy in a few days and will not sleep in the corner anyways. And then, once that surgery is done and I am recovered, it will be time for my skin grafts on my legs and then my double hip replacement. The following year will be nothing but surgery, pain, healing, pain, recovery and then start over at the beginning. So yeah, I guess my sleeping in the corner will come to an end soon enough.

I hear a knock on my door, and I look at my phone. Oh wow, I have been sitting here writing for an entire hour. Someone knocks again, and I clear my throat and say, "Come in!". I stand up slowly, as I am stiff from how I had been sitting for the last hour. The door opens slowly, and Rodriguez walks in. The first thing I notice is that he is using a cane to walk. I choke back the tears that are trying so hard to come out. I want to rush over to him and collapse into his arms, but I have to keep my strong act going.

He stops at the foot of my bed and stares at me. It occurs to me that he is looking at a ghost. I clear my throat. "Damn, Roddie, I'm not sure who looks older, you or me." My joke gets the reaction I was hoping for, and he laughs and looks up at the ceiling. "Sanders, you have no idea how long I have thought about this day." He looks back at me, and there are tears in his eyes. I realize that there is no point in the tough act with Roddie. He was my best friend for so long, and I can let down my guard for him. I walk over to him and go right in for a hug. He is shocked by the contact, as I'm sure the staff instructed him not to touch me first. Everyone is told this. Don't touch Emily unless she initiates it first. After a few seconds, he gently wraps his arms around me, and I lean in tighter to his chest.

"God, Sanders, you have no idea the guilt I have felt all these years. I know sorry is not enough, but dammit, I am so fucking sorry for leaving you." I can't pull away, not yet. I need to stay against his chest until I get my tears under control. My words come out muffled since I have my face turned into his chest. "There is no reason to apologize. Do you hear me, Roddie?"

Now I pull away from our embrace and look up into his eyes. His eyes are just as red as I am sure mine are. "Did you hear me, Roddie? You have nothing to be sorry about." He shakes his head and pulls away from me, and walks towards the window. "No, I should have saved you, dammit." I walk over to him and say, "It was you pulling on my arm, right? I could hear you and feel you pulling on my arm, but I couldn't respond. I was trapped in the Humvee."

"Yeah, that was me, and I left you there. I fucking listened to Simmons and left you there." He lets out a deep sigh, and his head sags on his shoulders. "Roddie, you need to let this go, okay? I do not hold you responsible for what happened, okay? Will it make it better if I say I forgive you?" At this, Roddie turns around and faces me. "Simmons is dead, Emily. He killed himself because of the guilt he carried. He couldn't handle the guilt any longer. Do you think I carry guilt? That dude died believing that it was all his fault that we left you and Grant behind."

I stand there in utter disbelief at what Roddie has just dropped on me. Simmons took his own life? What the hell? I back up and bump into my hospital bed and sit on the edge of it. This news explains why every time I brought up Roddie and Simmons that Josh would change the subject. He couldn't tell me about Simmons. Not after the fact that he had to be the one to confirm Grant was dead, and then the real topper had been him telling me that my dad had died of cancer. Simmons was fucking dead.

"Sanders, say something to me, please." Now it was Roddie's turn to walk over to me and stand in front of me. I shake my head and lick my lips before I reply. "Simmons is dead. Grant is dead. My dad is dead. Who else is dead, Roddie? Anyone else I need to know about?" Roddie shakes his head no, and that brings me some relief. Okay, maybe the worst of the news is behind us then. "Right, well then, catch me up on some good news, will you please?"

Roddie forces a smile and goes over to the chair I had been sitting in when he had arrived. I turn to face him, and he begins to tell me about his wife and the life they built after he was medically retired. He tells me how he kept in close contact with Josh and the girls all these years—never missing a birthday or special event. Tara especially was close to Roddie. She had confided in him when she was younger that she didn't believe that I was dead. He encouraged her to follow her dreams, and if Tara truly felt that way, she should see where her gut would take her. He said how Josh had no clue that he had been helping her and supported her all these years of additional tutoring she needed on Arabic, culture, history, and military history. When Tara had graduated from high school, he gave her some of my gear from Iraq.

We talked long enough that the staff brought lunch in for both of us, and we laughed over our food. Roddie joked that it was barely a step up from an MRE, and I reminded him that this was way better than what I had been eating. Even though I hadn't said that to make him feel bad, it hurt our time together; he stopped eating and looked out the window. "Look, Roddie, you have to find peace. I am here, and I am alive. Yes, I was a prisoner and went through some nasty shit, but I am here. We can't change the past; we can't keep chasing ghosts. The only thing we can do is...." "Move always forward." He cuts me off before I have time to complete my sentence, and we smile at each other.

There is another knock on the door, and Josh pokes his head in the door. Roddie picks up his hospital tray and stands up. "Damn, they let anyone in this hospital, don't they?" Josh says as he walks in the door. I reach out to him, and he grabs my left hand and squeezes it gently. I want to stand up and kiss him, but we are still in a weird place, considering he is married to another woman. Josh lets go of my hand, and he walks over to Roddie, and they hug. It makes me happy to know they have had each other all these years. Roddie truly was the best battle buddy a girl could have.

Chapter Eighteen

JOSH

———◇———

Walking in and seeing Roddie and Emily together was just what Josh needed to see. It had been a rough morning, talking to Dina. He knew Dina sensed things were not well between them, and she had offered to fly to D.C. to be there for Josh. Josh had cut her off and told her no. He didn't want to end their marriage over the phone. She deserved better than that. He told her he would be flying home in a few days before Emily's surgeries began. He planned on telling her then that he wanted a divorce.

Now, being here at the hospital, he knew he was taking the right steps. His heart was here with Emily. She was his soulmate, and he didn't want to leave her long enough to go back to North Carolina, but he had to get this over with Dina. When Emily reached for his hand, that sealed the deal.

"Damn, they let anyone in this hospital now?" Josh rags on Roddie as if this was any old meeting and not the first time Roddie was seeing Emily after thinking she had been dead for close to two decades. Roddie pulls Josh in for a hug and says, "Well, clearly, they let you in here, didn't they? That's not saying much, now, is it?" They both laugh and pull back from the hug.

Josh loved Roddie like a brother, so physical contact was not awkward for them at all.

Josh leans against the wall and crosses his arms. "From the looks of it, it seems like you two never missed a beat. Everything good here?" Josh looked back from Emily to Roddie. He knew both of them had been terrified about this reunion. Initially, Emily had requested Roddie be here when she was stateside. But then, once they had landed and everything was sinking in, she had asked to postpone the meeting. Of course, Roddie would wait. Everyone was following Emily's cues on everything from her treatment plans to her eating and sleeping schedule. The main goal with her recovery was to allow her to be in control. All of her doctors had told Josh and the girls that. With how long she had been in captivity, she needed complete control over what was happening to her now. And Josh understood that. He would give her all the control and space she would need in the upcoming months, shit, even years.

Roddie nods his head and looks down at the floor. Emily clears her throat and speaks. "Yeah, we are good to go, right, Roddie?" Roddie looks up and smiles at Emily and then Josh, "G to G– it's the only way to be!" They all bust out laughing, as that was something Roddie always used to say when Emily would ask him if he was good. Josh shook his head and kept laughing. Listening to them talking felt good and easy. He kept waiting for the difficult days to show up. He had been reading more and more on severe cases of PTSD, and Emily wasn't showing any signs of it. It was like she was bouncing back with no issues at all.

"Roddie, we are going to head to the cemetery soon; you want to come with us?" Josh scans both Emily and Roddie before Roddie has a chance to speak up. "No, man, that's a trip for you two. I will be here for a few more days, and I will be back." Roddie fist bumps

Josh and then walks over to Emily. Emily stands up and goes right in for the hug with Roddie. Seeing these two together made him so happy. Watching Roddie all these years beat himself up over Emily, Grant and even Simmons was hard to watch. Roddie keeps a hold on Emily and talks to the top of her head, "And when I come back, I am bringing you some real food. No more of this bullshit hospital crap. He gently kisses the top of Emily's head, and Emily steps back and is beaming from ear to ear. "Sounds like a plan, Specialist Rodriguez. Just don't be late." She gives him a nudge in the side, and he pretends to wince in pain. "Roger that, Sarge. Roger that!"

Josh walks Roddie to the door, and they exchange one more hug, and then Roddie is gone. Josh looks back to Emily, who has sat back on the bed. "Hey, are you good to go? Do you want to take a nap before we head out? I have all the time in the world." Emily smiles at him, "You know, a nap does sound pretty fantastic right about now. Let me just get in a quick ten-minute shut-eye, okay?"

Josh nods his head and turns to leave, but Emily stops him. "Wait, you can stay here if you want. That way, you can wake me up if I go past the ten minutes." Josh smiled and was hoping she would ask him to stay. "You got it. I will make sure to wake up if you start to snore." Emily throws a pillow at Josh. "I DO NOT SNORE, JOSH SANDERS!" He laughs and picks up the pillow and gently props it up behind her head. He smooths the hair away from her face and gets lost in her green eyes. "Sweet dreams Emily Sanders."

Chapter Nineteen

EMILY

The entire drive to Arlington has been surreal. I still cannot believe that I'm safe. I keep waiting for the monster to return. Any moment now, I am going to wake up, and he will be standing over me. This can't be real. The SUV slows down, and I look out the window and see we are entering the cemetery. I remember in another lifetime coming here for the changing of the guards. This place is so sad without having a personal connection to it. But here we are, coming to visit my own grave. Part of me feels so bad for forcing Josh to bring me here. But I need to do this. I need to see my grave and Grant's. Eventually, I will need to get to Simmons, now that I know the truth about what happened to him as well.

I feel those nagging pains in my stomach and roll down the window for some fresh air. The August air is warm, and the wind nips at my cheeks. I inhale deeply through my nose and close my eyes. I try not to think about the news Roddie just dropped on me this morning. Simmons is dead because of his guilt over losing Grant and me. I realize the pain I am feeling is for him, his family, and Roddie. I wish Josh would have told me sooner. Roddie should not have had to carry the weight of telling me about Simmons.

Josh looks over to me as he slowly turns down one of the avenues. "You sure you are ready for this? We can still turn around; it's not too late." He puts his right hand on the gear shifter, which is his signal that if I want to hold his hand, I can. I know the doctors have been working with him when he is not with me. I know they are telling him not to touch me without my consent and take it slow. The funny thing is, I'm not scared of him touching me because of my past. I don't want to begin feeling those feelings again because he's married to another woman. I smile at him and pat the top of his hand. "I'm good, Josh. I need to see my grave. I even snuck out a sharpie so I can cross out the deceased date." The look on Josh's face is priceless. "Josh Sanders, you know I am not serious!" I laugh, and then he shakes his head and begins to laugh too. He slows down more and pulls the SUV over, close to the edge of the lane. He puts the SUV into park and turns off the engine.

"So, this is it, huh? We are here." The last part is a statement more than a question. He looks down at the keys in his hand and nods his yes. This time, I do reach over and place my hand on his. He looks up at me with tears in his eyes. God, I am a selfish person to make him bring me here. He had to bury me here, and now he's bringing me here alive.

"Josh, if you want to stay here, just point me in the right direction, and I am sure I can find it on my own." He shakes his head and blinks back the tears. "No, this is just as much for you as it is for me. I need this too." With that, we both exit the SUV, Josh rushing over to my side to help me out. As much as I don't want him to help me, I take his help. It isn't easy getting in and out of these SUVs.

When my hip replacements and the rest of the surgeries are behind me, I look forward to the future. I want to be independent again. Once I am out and steady, Josh gently touches my elbow, and I smile at him to know that this is okay. He guides me into the sea of gravestones, all in their uniform rows. Each stone is the same as the next; the only difference is the names, ranks, religious symbols, and dates. We walk about halfway down the row, and Josh stops. His face loses all color, and for a moment, I think I might be the one that needs to steady him.

"Remember my motto Josh Sanders; we only move forward. Always forward." He nods his head, and I switch my cane to my left hand and link my right arm through his left arm. He looks down at me, more than likely shocked that I have initiated human contact with him twice in less than one hour. He nods his head in the direction of the gravestone directly in front of him. "There it is. Sgt. Emily Sanders, rest in peace." He closes his eyes, and I can tell he can't stop the tears from falling this time. I unlink my arm from his and slowly walk towards the grave.

There it is. Sgt. Emily Sanders' gravestone. As I look down at it, I feel completely disconnected from what is happening at this moment. I can hear Josh sniffling behind me, trying to hold back more tears, yet I feel nothing. I don't feel sad. I don't feel angry. I feel absolutely nothing. I look at the top of the stone marker, and there is a collection of pennies, nickels, dimes, and even a quarter. I close my eyes and wonder who left which coin. Pennies could be from anyone that has been here; a nickel could be any of the few hundred soldiers I trained with in basic training. But the dimes and the lonely quarter are what have me curious. A dime means the person served with me, and the quarter means they were there when I died. I died. I died, and one of the soldiers from my unit on the mission came here to pay their respects.

Now I begin to feel something. I feel a burning rage coming from the ground below my feet. Perhaps the anger is bubbling up from the empty coffin that is buried six feet deep below me. Maybe it is the fact that I was left behind in that burning Humvee and was left to die. Whatever it is, the rage keeps coming, and I don't think about the words that come out of my mouth next.

"You all left me to die. You all left me behind and buried an empty coffin." I do not turn to face Josh; I keep staring down at my gravestone. "I died. I died, and everyone gave up on me. Everyone but my sweet little four-year-old daughter. She was the only one brave enough to chase a ghost her entire life." At this, I turn around and face Josh. But he is looking down at the ground, tears quietly falling from his eyes. I know I shouldn't yell at him like this, but I can't stop the rage from continuing. I turn back around, and the sight of all those coins on my gravestone brings a new wave of rage. I take my right hand and swipe all the coins off of the grave. Some fall to the ground, some bounce off the grave next to mine. I pound my fist into the top of the marker.

I continue to pound my fist into the gravestone and hear this wailing and howling, and it occurs to me that it is me making those sounds. I fall to my knees and continue to cry; they left me there to die. Everyone left me to die. I feel Josh kneel behind me, and he begins to wrap his arms around me. "DO NOT TOUCH ME!!" I scream as loud as I can. I struggle to push myself back up and have to use my gravestone to help me stand up. I wipe my eyes and take a deep breath. I do not turn around when I begin to speak next because I can't bear to see Josh's reaction to what I am about to say.

"Josh, I know you love me, and I know you truly did everything you could to find me. But right now, I am struggling with all of this." I sweep my hand, motioning to the thousands of graves around me. "I am struggling with being alive. I am struggling with being dead. I am struggling with what you need from me." I hear him take a sharp inhale, bracing himself for what I am about to say. "I love you, Josh Sanders, but I can't be your wife right now. I need to figure out how the hell to be alive again, and I need to do that on my own." I pause and take a deep breath before I speak my peace. "I want you to go back to North Carolina and be with Dina, your current wife."

As I say those final words, I slowly turn around, and now Josh is looking me dead in the eyes. "Emily Sanders, I never stopped loving you, and deep down, I wanted to believe you were alive. I understand you're angry, and you have every single right to be. And I will go back to North Carolina, but rest assured, I will be back. I don't need anything from you. I don't need you to love me or be my wife. But I want to be here to help you. So, I will go back home, but I will be back." And with that, Josh turns around and walks back to the SUV. He gets in and leans his head back against the headrest, and closes his eyes.

I turn back to look at my name engraved in the stone one more time. The raging storm has moved on as quickly as it came in. All that is left is regret and remorse in my heart. I feel terrible for saying what I just said, but I can't take back those words. They were, after all, the truth. I look to the ground where the coins fell and look to the gravestone to the right of mine. And that is when the name registers to me, Specialist Edward Grant. I close my eyes, and I pick up one of the quarters, and I gently place it on the top of his cold stone. I kiss my fingers and then put them on his name. I whisper to Grant, "I am so sorry, bud.

You were too good of a man to die so young, but I think you may have been the lucky one. Right now, I kind of wish I was lying in the grave next to you."

I slowly make my way back to the SUV, and I notice Josh stays in his seat. Good, I need to start doing things on my own; I can't rely on him or anyone else. I need to figure out this new life of mine. I understand that everyone feels they owe me something, but I don't want their help right now. They need to let me start anew.

We drive back to the hospital in silence. I stare out the window, taking in all the sights around me. Sometimes it can still be overwhelming to see the changing landscape when I was used to the desert for so long. Josh pulls into the parking lot and finds a spot relatively close to the front entrance. After he puts the SUV in park and turns off the ignition, he places both hands on the steering wheel and lets out a long sigh.

Before he has a chance to speak his mind, I have to say my peace. "Josh, I know you love me, and I love you too. But you are married to another woman, and I know you love her too. And although it's difficult for me to understand, I need you to go back to her. You need to sort out your life with her, and I need to sort out my life." I pause, but I raise my hand to him so he knows I have more to say. "You will always be my one and only, but right now, I have to get through these surgeries and recovery without worrying about you and Dina. The girls will stay here with me, and my mom will be here to help me too. You only serve to add more stress to my recovery, and even though that is not your intention, that is honest to god truth." I drop my hand into my lap, and I continue to look at Josh's profile as he stares straight ahead.

A single tear rolls down his cheek, and he wipes it away before turning to look at me. "Emily, as much as

I want to fight you on this and scream to the heavens how much I love you, I know deep down how much you need this. As far as Dina goes, I am divorcing her because the truth is that you were and are my one and only soul mate. I will hold the regret for the rest of my life that I gave up on you. And even though I may not be able to accept it, I understand that you do not want me here right now. But know this, Emily Sanders, I will check on you daily with the girls, even if you don't hear from me. I love you with my entire being and will do whatever it takes to get you back to me."

With that, Josh takes his right hand off the steering wheel and places his hand palm up on the console between us. I put my left hand on top and squeezed his hand. I can't bring myself to kiss him, even though I want to so badly. He squeezes back gently, and then I release my hand. Before he can have the chance to help me back into the hospital, I get out and walk away from him in the parking lot. I'm terrified to do this without him, but I need to start my new life on my terms. The surgeries will be hell, and the recovery will be too, but nothing, and I mean nothing, can be worse than the hell I have already lived. No more living in the past, I am only moving forward, and I will come back stronger than ever.

Acknowledgments

I want to begin by thanking everyone that read the first book, Always Forward. I learned a lot through writing and publishing Always Forward, and feedback from the readers has been vital in my continued writing and publishing of Chasing Ghosts. Like Always Forward, more people than I can list have been there for me throughout this journey. But I will do my best to highlight a few.

To my beta readers who continue to take time out of their busy lives to read Chasing Ghosts, thank you from the bottom of my heart for sticking with me through this process and continuing to give me ideas and constructive criticism.

To my sisters, Nora and Carol, thank you for always being my biggest cheerleaders over the years. And to my brother, Nick, I will never forget our trip to Florida or when you bought every item on my deployment packing list. Sometimes we say 'I love you' a little differently in our family. From taking care of me as an annoying little sister to supporting me during my time in the military, and to now cheering me on from afar, none of it has gone unnoticed. The bond between siblings is unbreakable, and I hope you all know how much I love each of you.

My daughters, Alesandra and Annalecia- you both continue to support me in this process, helping me with book sales and being my sounding board when I have new ideas. Thank you for staying true to yourselves and for your bond to each other. Again, the bond between siblings is strong with you two, even if you drive each other crazy sometimes.

Finally, to my better half, Milo. If I thought before Always Forward, you were my rock, well, you have proven that you continue to be rock steady. I know it has not been easy to deal with the writing and publishing process, but you have been there for me every step of the way. You keep me calm when all I want to do is stress out, and you help me remain level-headed when things are out of my control. Always Forward and Chasing Ghosts are just as much your labors of love as they are mine. I love you more than you can ever know.

About the Author

Cecilia A. Garcia is a combat veteran, having served eight years in the Army. While deployed to Iraq in 2004, Emily's story came alive, and it took close to seventeen years to share Always Forward finally, and now Chasing Ghosts with the world. While serving in Iraq, Garcia was injured by a roadside bomb. She has spent the last seventeen years working through her traumas while trying to break the stigma for veterans living with PTSD and traumatic brain injuries.

Garcia has been married to her husband and fellow soldier for the last twenty-one years. They have two daughters, Alesandra and Annalecia. Now that her daughters are older, Garcia loves to spoil her five pets, also known as the creative team behind the author. She has three dogs– Sajar, Stella, Nappy, and two cats– Hero and Mishka.

When Garcia is not writing, walking the dogs, or spending time with her family, she loves to be in her gardens, running, or practicing yoga. She has plans to continue writing the Always Forward series and other series, including characters from Always

Forward and Chasing Ghosts. To learn more, check out www.authorceciliagarcia.com.

Made in the USA
Middletown, DE
23 January 2022

59460779R00076